The idea of Dane touching her made her more nervous than she thought possible.

He lifted a brow. "It's either I check you out or we take you to the doctor."

"Okay, check."

He pressed his large hands to her rib cage under her loose top. Her breathing had gone shallow. It had been almost a year since she'd been with a man. But she'd only known this man less than a day. He was a stranger. A very dangerous stranger.

Yet, emotion and desire overruled reason. She'd been alone for so long and she wanted to feel connected to someone, if only for a short while.

Sensing the first move would have to be hers, she rose up on tiptoes and gently kissed his lips.

Dear Reader,

Yoga is one of my passions and for the past four years I've been a dedicated student. During yoga classes my mind often wanders off to that quiet place where my stories are born. It was during a yoga class that I caught my first glimpses of Kristen and Dane, the heroine and hero of *Wise Moves,* which of course is set in a yoga studio. Kristen and Dane begin their journey as lost souls, but despite it all they bravely face the threats in the physical world. Their reward is inner peace that allows each to love the other.

I hope *Wise Moves* keeps you on the edge of your seat, touches your heart and for just a little while takes you away from the hectic pace of the outer world.

Have a safe and happy summer!

Mary Burton

MARY BURTON
WISE
MOVES

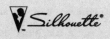

INTIMATE MOMENTS™

Published by Silhouette Books

America's Publisher of Contemporary Romance

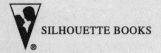 SILHOUETTE BOOKS

ISBN-13: 978-0-373-27496-3
ISBN-10:   0-373-27496-3

WISE MOVES

Books by Mary Burton

Silhouette Intimate Moments

In Dark Waters #1378
The Arsonist #1410
Wise Moves #1426

Harlequin Historicals

A Bride for McCain #502
The Colorado Bride #570
The Perfect Wife #614
Christmas Gold #627
  "Until Christmas"
Rafferty's Bride #632
The Lightkeeper's Woman #693
The Unexpected Wife #708
Heart of the Storm #757

MARY BURTON

sold her first novel in 1999 and since then has written eight Harlequin Historical novels. *Wise Moves* is her third contemporary novel for Silhouette Intimate Moments. Burton not only enjoys a variety of hobbies, including yoga, hiking and scuba diving, but also recently tackled her first triathlon. A graduate of Hollins University, she is based in Richmond, Virginia, where she lives with her husband and two children.

Prologue

Danger surrounded Elena Benito.

The dark sensation had grown steadily since she'd returned to Miami yesterday, winding her nerves tighter than a drum. At 9:00 a.m., just six hours from now, she was scheduled to testify against her brother, drug kingpin Antonio Benito.

Unable to sleep, Elena paced the small furnished room of the FBI's Dade County safe house. Feeling trapped, she sat on the twin bed, picked up the TV remote, clicked on the small television and started surfing. But none of the B-movies, late-night talk shows or infomercials distracted her from her fears.

Her brother was out there, looking for her, and he wanted to punish her.

She clicked off the television. The house's old air-conditioning system couldn't overcome the hot, humid July air, making it difficult to breathe.

Rising, Elena flexed and released her fingers. She had to get out of this room.

She opened her bedroom door, which fed into the living room furnished with bamboo furniture and a green shag carpet. Flowery drapes covered a large picture window by the wooden front door.

This room felt as foreign as the safe house in New Mexico where the FBI had hidden her. Out west, she'd dreamed of getting out of the mountains and returning to the Miami she loved. She longed for her beloved beaches and the sight of the ocean. But now as she stared around this seedy house, she realized the Miami she'd loved was lost to her forever.

Police officers Jack Mendez and Nancy Rogers were the Miami officers assigned to guard Elena until the FBI detail picked her up at seven. The police officers' voices and the click of cards shuffling drifted out from the kitchen.

Both Rogers and Mendez had called this operation a routine gig, but there was nothing routine about any of this. The officers, like everyone else involved in her brother's murder trial, knew how much rode on her testimony. The Feds had been after Antonio for years. But they'd never been able to pin anything on him until Elena had told police she'd witnessed her brother kill six members of a local Miami church.

The "Churchmen," as they were known by the press, had effectively stopped the drug trade in their neighborhood with peaceful sit-ins and a neighborhood watch program. Angered by sagging profits, Antonio had decided to send all he knew a message by murdering the men. He'd forced Elena to witness the killings because she, too, was being taught a lesson: Never run from me again.

Elena had begged for the lives of the men, but Antonio had showed no mercy and shot each in cold blood. It had taken her another nineteen days before she'd found another opportunity to escape Antonio. This time, when she ran, she had gone to the police. She had identified her brother as the shooter and he had been arrested.

She moved silently through the house to the open kitchen door. Mendez stood at the kitchen sink as a coffeepot brewed. His white Guayabera shirt accentuated rich brown skin. "My old lady was talking about buying a bigger house."

Nancy sat at a yellow Formica kitchen table and shuffled a worn deck of cards. The room's pineapple wallpaper and appliances dated back to the fifties. "Her high-dollar tastes are gonna break you, Mendez."

Mendez's full mustache twitched when he smiled. "Nah, I can handle her."

Nancy dealt two hands. "That's what they all say."

Floorboards under Elena's feet squeaked as she crossed the threshold. Immediately the officers' gazes whipped around. Nancy was already reaching for her gun.

Elena rubbed smooth hands over designer jeans. "I'm sorry. I just wanted a glass of water."

Nancy clipped her gun back in the holster and smiled. "Sure."

"I'll get it," Mendez said.

As Mendez filled a glass with tap water, Nancy stood. "Is everything in your room okay?"

Elena hugged her arms around her chest. "It's fine."

There was softness in Nancy Rogers's eyes when she nodded. "It will all be over soon."

Elena tried to take comfort from the officer's words, but found the ominous dread in her would not stop growing. "Yes."

"You're doing the right thing," Nancy said. "Your brother is a monster and he needs to be put away."

Elena had never expected that doing the right thing would be so hard. "It's what must be done."

A sound from the street caught Nancy's attention. "Did you hear something?"

Mendez shut the tap off and set the glass on the counter. He peaked through the kitchen's miniblinds. "Looks like the transfer team arrived early."

Elena's fingers trembled as she pushed back the cuff of her silk blouse and checked the Rolex on her slim wrist. "They're four hours early." She suddenly felt cold, as if Death had brushed past her.

Nancy's hand slid to the holster clipped to her jeans. "I don't like it."

"He's here," Elena whispered as she stepped back. She hated being afraid, being a coward. "He's come to kill me."

Nancy shook her head, puzzled by Elena's words. "Who? Antonio? He's not here."

Elena shook her head, unable to deny the feelings in her. "He's sent people to kill me."

"Don't borrow trouble, Ms. Benito. It could be nothing," Nancy said.

Instinct whispered differently.

Nancy switched off the living room light and moved past Elena into the dark room. She peeked out thick curtains covering the picture window. "It makes sense they'd change the schedule. I just wish they'd told us."

There was no tension in Mendez's face when he came into the living room and looked out the same window. A gold signet ring on his pinky caught the moonlight. "Varying the pickup time just means tighter security, Ms. Benito. The car looks like Miami D.A. issue. No need to worry."

Nancy flipped open her cell phone. The light of its screen cast a faint blue light on her angled faced. "I'm calling the lieutenant to see if this is legit."

Mendez rubbed the back of his neck. "Man, I hope this gig *is* ending four hours early. I haven't slept in my own bed in two nights and I'm missing my old lady's loving."

Elena stepped back toward her room. She glanced at the side window in her bedroom that led to a back alley.

"Remember the plan," Nancy said to Elena as if reading her thoughts. "If there is any trouble, climb out the window. There is a car parked in the alley. Keys are under the mat and the gas tank is full. Go straight to the central office."

Mendez looked surprised. "Who put the car out back?"

"I did. Just in case," Nancy said.

He cracked his knuckles. "You're so anal, Rogers."

"Better anal than dead, as my brother says," Nancy shot back.

Elena didn't want to be a coward, but raw fear churned in her gut. "Do *you* think it's Antonio?"

Nancy looked calm, too calm, as if she didn't want to spook her witness. She held her phone close to her ear. "Chances are it's like Mendez said. They've changed the pickup time."

Mendez moved toward the door. "You two are worrying over nothing. It's FBI. This time tomorrow Benito will be in—"

Nancy snapped her fingers, signaling Mendez to stop talking as someone came on the line. "Hello, Lt. Grasser, this is Officer Rogers at the Benito safe house. I need a confirmation on an early pickup. We've got men who look like FBI in our driveway now. Right. Okay." She muttered an oath. "The guy put me on hold."

There was a loud knock at the front door. "Mendez and Rogers open up. FBI."

Mendez looked through the peephole. "He's holding up a FBI badge." He reached for the handle.

"Don't open that door!" Nancy shouted. "Wait until I get a confirmation."

Mendez smiled at his partner.

Elena froze. His was the same oily smile she'd seen on Antonio's face before he'd killed the Churchmen.

Elena felt sick. "He's going to betray us."

Shock registered on Nancy's face but before she could react, Mendez turned the deadbolt.

"Mendez, don't," Nancy shouted.

"I've got to," he said. "There's five million on *her* head and I want it."

The shock on Nancy's face gave way to anger in a split second. Dropping her cell phone, Nancy reached for her gun and shot Mendez in the leg before he could open the door.

"Run!" Nancy shouted to Elena.

Frozen with fear, Elena watched Mendez drop to his knees.

"Bitch." Wincing, Mendez reached for the door-knob.

"Run!" Nancy shouted again to Elena.

Elena did not want to leave the officer behind. She liked the woman and knew if Nancy stayed she'd die.

"Come with me!" Elena begged.

"No," Nancy said. "Now go!"

Elena felt like a coward as she ran into the bed-room. Her high heels caught in the shag carpet and she stumbled to the floor by her bed.

Behind her, she heard the crack of wood splinter-ing as the front door slammed open. Her heart ham-mering, she kicked off her shoes, rose and ran toward the window. She jerked back the curtains and fumbled with the lock.

Elena glanced back as Nancy swung around, her Beretta raised as three men entered the house. One pulled a sawed-off double-barreled shotgun from under his black suit jacket. He shot Mendez point-blank in the head. The policeman dropped to the floor, dead.

Nancy fired and hit the shooter in the chest. He fell back into the wall and slid to the floor.

Elena said a silent prayer as she fumbled with the window's lock. She and Nancy had reviewed the escape plan just hours ago, but her thoughts tripped inside her head.

More gunshots exploded in the living room.

The lock gave way and the window opened. Elena hoisted herself up onto the sill and swung her legs over. She jumped the four feet to the soft ground. Bare feet sunk in the moist dirt.

Nancy screamed, firing again. The agonizing sounds tore at Elena. Another shot exploded and then silence.

Elena didn't have to see to know that Officer Nancy Rogers was dead.

Tears clouded her eyes and she ran to the car. Nancy had sacrificed herself for Elena. With trembling hands she opened the car door. The dome light flashed on and she reached under the front mat and got the keys. She immediately closed the door. The vehicle plunged into darkness.

In her rush, she dropped the keys on the floor. Frantically, she ran her hand along the carpeted floor until she felt the cold metal of the keys.

Inside the house, two men entered her room and went to the window out of which she'd just climbed. She shoved the key into the ignition and turned on the engine.

Elena didn't dare look back at the house for fear she'd see them coming. She put the car in Drive and sped down the side street.

Tonight had proven that the five-million-dollar reward on her head was enough to turn anyone against her, including the police. If she showed up at the courthouse later this morning, she would die. Antonio would see to it.

Her heart ached for Nancy. The officer deserved justice. The Churchmen deserved justice.

There was nothing she could do for any of them now but disappear.

Chapter 1

Nine Months Later, Tuesday, April 24, 11:00 a.m.

As Kristen Rodale approached the small town's historic district, asphalt and nondescript buildings gave way to tree-lined cobblestone streets and turn-of-the-century buildings with flower boxes in the windows.

A gold-leaf sign on a wooden post near a courthouse with white columns read, Welcome.

Welcome.

It had been so long since she'd felt welcome. So long since she'd felt wanted, nurtured and loved. But close contact with anyone was too dangerous. Not only did the police want her, but her brother Antonio wanted her as well.

Two old men stood in front of an antique shop, glanced up and nodded as she passed. Reflex had her stiffening, and it took a concerted effort to relax her shoulders and nod a greeting back.

Nine months of running and still she didn't like being scrutinized.

She shifted her backpack to the other shoulder, strolling past a delightful collection of stores. A lingerie shop, an Italian restaurant with a collection of sidewalk tables, a high-end clothing store—each was as unique and special as the century-old stone buildings that housed them. Two years ago—a lifetime ago—she would have shopped in stores like these and never have glanced at a price tag. Now pennies were precious.

A coffee shop's large picture window caught her attention. Tucked in the first floor of an old redbrick bank building, the shop was stuffed with a collection of small round tables, an old jukebox and bin after bin of specialty coffees. The rich sights lured her closer.

She thought about the money in her pocket. She'd saved five hundred dollars by scrimping and saving. Her goal was to buy a car, so that she wouldn't have to rely on buses and trains where anyone could recognize her.

As she entered the shop, bells jingled above her head and a rush of warm air greeted her. Most of the tables were filled with mothers chatting to other mothers as their babies gurgled in wooden high chairs, tourists with cameras and maps and a worker grabbing a coffee, presumably before her afternoon shift.

Kristen studied the menu. She could have splurged on a preferred cappuccino but decided on a much less expensive small coffee and a muffin.

She walked to the ancient cash register where a young man with a crop of red hair stood. "What'll it be?"

She cleared her throat. It had been days since she'd spoken to anyone. "Small coffee, in a regular to-go cup, and a blueberry muffin."

"Coming right up." He poured her the coffee and set it on the counter and then plated up the muffin.

She counted out quarters, dimes and pennies to the right amount. "Thanks."

As he rang up her purchase and counted her change, he asked, "You passing through?"

She sipped her coffee. Delicious warmth spread to her chilled fingers. "I was thinking about staying a while." She dumped fifty cents in the tip jar. Having lived off tips these past nine months she knew how the extra coins could add up.

The young man nodded his thanks. "Cool. You'll like it here. I'm Pete, what's your name?"

This question always brought a moment's hesitation. For the first eight months on the run, she'd changed her name often, fearing she would be traced. But this last month, she'd grown confident as she'd become more streetwise. She'd settled on the name "Kristen," and announced this to Pete.

"Kristen. Welcome."

"Thanks."

"So are you looking for a job?"

"Yes. Know of any?"

Another customer came into the store. "I think so. Let me take care of this guy first."

"Sure."

As Pete waited on the new customer, Kristen took an empty seat by the large picture window and settled her backpack between her feet. Sunlight streamed in. She closed her eyes and savored the warmth on her skin.

If there was one thing she missed most about her old life, it was the sun. She'd grown up accustomed to bathing suits, the scent of sun screen, sandals and sleeveless dresses.

She ate her muffin. It was a bit dry but sitting at a table and eating off of a real plate made it palatable.

The muffin gone, she was savoring her coffee when the bells on the front door rang again. A cool breeze flowed into the shop on the heels of a slender woman with shoulder-length blond hair. She wore a loose-fitting black turtleneck sweater that topped a green peasant skirt. Sporting well-worn Birkenstocks on her feet, she moved through the room as if she didn't have a care in the world.

"Good morning, Pete!" she called out.

Pete stood a little straighter and grinned. "Morning, Sheridan. You want the regular soy latte?"

"Yes, thank you." She tossed a five on the counter. "So how is your mom? I hear she's out of the hospital."

"She's good. The cast should come off in a couple of weeks."

"That's wonderful. Have her come by the Yoga Studio when she's feeling better. I'll show her some moves to limber up. She's going to be stiff."

"Thanks, I will." He handed her the latte in a porcelain cup and made change.

Carelessly, she dumped the couple dollars' worth of change in the tip jar and grabbed two packets of sugar from the counter.

"Oh, hey, are you still looking for a receptionist?" Pete said.

Sheridan's eyes brightened. "Yes."

"Well, that gal over there is new in town and looking for work."

It took a second for Kristen to realize Pete was talking about her. Immediately, she tensed.

Sheridan settled her gaze on Kristen. Shrewd eyes studied her before she strolled toward Kristen's table.

"So, is my young friend correct?" Sheridan said. "Are you looking for a job?"

Rising, Kristen cleared her throat. Sheridan stood a good five inches taller than her own five-foot-two inches, but Kristen kept her chin high and her gaze direct. "I am."

"My name is Sheridan Young."

"Kristen Rodale."

"Mind if I sit down?"

"Sure." As the two sat, she reminded herself that she had no reason to be nervous. She'd had a dozen jobs in the past nine months. Besides, she'd survived hell and lived to tell the tale.

"What brings you to Lancaster Springs?"

"I like to travel."

"So you won't be staying long."

Kristen heard the apprehension in the woman's voice. "I like this town. I could easily stay here." That was the truth. If she could stay, she would.

Sheridan dumped raw sugar into her coffee and stirred it. "Your breathing is shallow."

"What?"

"Shallow. You don't take deep breaths. Is it habit or stress?"

Behind the easygoing appearance was a shrewd woman. "Habit, I suppose."

"I'd vote stress."

Kristen picked up her coffee and sipped as her thoughts stumbled. Sheridan didn't know her from Adam. And there were millions of reasons why people got stressed out. "Why do you say that?"

"The breathing and your eyes give it away."

Kristen blinked. Maybe this *wasn't* the town for her.

As if reading her mind, Sheridan smiled. "Don't look so nervous. I'm not going to dig too deep."

Kristen nodded and, more to change the subject, said, "You said something about a job?"

"As a matter of fact I did. I own the Yoga Studio. Up until now I've been all the help I could afford, but the studio is doing well and I'm looking to hire a receptionist. I pay seven dollars an hour."

"It sounds great," Kristen said honestly.

"But…"

Kristen managed to keep her face blank. "What makes you think there is a but?"

Sheridan rose. "Pete, mind if I take this mug? I'll bring it back in a couple of hours."

Pete raised his hand. "No problemo."

Sheridan hitched her head toward the door. "Get your cup. Walk with me."

Kristen wasn't sure what to say but picked up her cup, hoisted her backpack on her shoulder and followed Sheridan down the tree-lined street.

They walked several blocks north of the historical district into a neighborhood that hadn't been renovated yet. In the center of the aging buildings was a tall house made of gray stone. It had a red front door flanked by large pots filled with purple and yellow winter pansies. A sign painted in a breezy style hung above the door. It read: Yoga Studio. The building had a warm, calming quality.

"This is your place?"

"Yes." Pride was evident.

"It's lovely."

"I've worked hard to fix her up. She was a mess and marked for demolition when I bought her three years ago. But I could see there was still a good bit of life here. There's more work to be done, but I'm making progress."

"You like to rescue things," Kristen said as she stared at ivy trailing out of the window boxes.

A smile tugged at Sheridan's full mouth. "And you are good at sizing people up."

A necessary skill. "Yes."

Sheridan studied her. "There's sadness in your soul, Kristen Rodale."

Kristen felt the blood drain from her face. "Sadness isn't a crime is it?"

Sheridan sipped her coffee. "No, it's not. But someone as young as you shouldn't be so sad."

"No one ever said life was supposed to be happy."

A cloud passed in front of Sheridan's eyes. Kristen had hit a nerve. But just as soon as the sorrow appeared, it vanished. "Like I said, I pay seven dollars an hour and I also have a room above the studio, which you can use. I lived in the apartment until a couple of months ago. Now I live down the street in the youth shelter."

"Why the shelter?"

"The old director quit unexpectedly and they needed someone to run the place. I like the kids so for now it's my home."

"More people to save?"

"I suppose." Sheridan broke Kristen's gaze and let it travel over her building. "The apartment is yours if you want it, though I'll expect you to open the shop each morning by eight. That'll save me from having to arrive much before the 9:00 a.m. class. The shelter has a 10:00 p.m. curfew, but I never seem to get to bed before midnight."

Life had made Kristen cautious, skeptical of

lucky breaks. Sheridan just seemed too good to be true. "Why me?"

She lifted a brow. "Why hire you? Can't say. A gut feeling. Sometimes you have to be willing to take a chance on the unknown."

Sheridan was offering a job and a place to stay— a rare and wonderful combination. Kristen had purchased a social security number in Atlanta two months ago, so the paperwork wouldn't be an issue. It would be nice to call one place home for a while. And Lancaster Springs seemed like the last place Antonio would ever look for her.

Sheridan seemed to sense she'd not quite convinced Kristen. "Oh, did I mention the apartment has a microwave and small fridge?"

Here she could save more money. If she were careful she could save up enough for a car in a matter of months. "Sounds like heaven."

"It's nothing fancy, but it is clean and safe."

Safe.

There was a time when Kristen had believed she'd never be truly safe again, which was why she'd crisscrossed the country and still kept a thousand miles between herself and Florida. Hiding had become her specialty.

Yes, to stop moving was risky, but she'd covered her tracks well.

She was safe.

Kristen held out a hand to Sheridan. "I'll take your job."

The woman's grip was firm. "Good."

Chapter 2

Tuesday, April 24, 2:33 p.m.

Dane Cambia checked his watch. He itched to get this meeting going.

A week ago, he'd contacted Lucian Moss, a UCLA dropout who ran a company that specialized in computer security systems. Other corporations hired Moss to test the integrity of their networks. So far, there hadn't been a system he couldn't hack into.

The front door of the pub opened and Cambia recognized Lucian Moss from the last day of the

Antonio Benito trial. He remembered Lucian's anguished outcry when the "Innocent" verdict had been read. Moss's uncle had been among the Churchmen murdered in Miami last year.

The computer expert wore a Grateful Dead shirt, an old black leather jacket, faded jeans and scuffed leather boots. Thick black hair brushed broad muscled shoulders, making him look more like a Hell's Angel than a computer geek.

Cambia rose, waved him over. The men shook hands and sat down.

A waitress came and took Lucian's coffee order. If she thought Moss looked out of place in the tony Washington pub, she showed no sign of it.

Cambia waited until she'd delivered Lucian's coffee and topped off his mug. "Thanks for coming."

"Sure." He pushed his coffee aside.

Dane lowered his voice. "We share a common enemy."

Moss twisted an onyx ring on his pinky finger. "Really?"

"Antonio Benito."

Hatred darkened Moss's eyes. "What's Benito done to you?"

"My sister was Nancy Rogers, a Miami cop assigned to guard Elena Benito. The safe house was hit by gunmen. My sister was killed."

Lucian's dark eyes softened. "I'm sorry."

Sadness tightened around Dane's heart. He'd listened to the tape of Nancy's last conversation with her commanding officer twenty times. Her voice had been tense, tight and her shock clear when she'd realized her partner had betrayed them. Nancy had ordered Elena to run before firing her gun. It sliced at his gut every time.

"I need your help," Dane said.

"How so?"

"I've had people on the street looking for Elena Benito for six months. No one can find her. But I've heard you can find anybody."

"I can." The softly spoken words radiated confidence.

"I want to use Elena as bait," Dane said. "She's the only one Antonio Benito truly cares about, the only one that can flush him out."

Moss studied him. "The police failed to protect her before."

"*I* won't."

Lucian tapped a long finger on the table. "I did a little checking on you. Special Forces. A month ago you resigned from the FBI."

"That's right."

"Why'd you leave?"

"The law had their chance with Benito. Now it's my turn."

"You are going to kill him?"

"Yep."

For a moment Lucian said nothing and Dane feared he wasn't up for such hands-on work. "I want in on the kill."

Surprised, he sat back in his seat. "No."

"I've spent the last year going after Benito's finances. Most of his business is cash and handled off the books. But about thirty percent of it funnels through computers. I've taken all of that. It's driving Benito crazy and I know he'll kill me if he finds me." The threat of death did not seem to faze him. "But no matter how much money I take, it's never enough. I want him dead."

Dane understood the anger Lucian felt. "This is a little more hands-on than stealing electronic files from one thousand miles away."

Lucian's gaze didn't waver. "I know what I'm getting into, Cambia."

The last thing he needed was a John Wayne wanna-be getting himself killed or mucking up his show. "This is *my* operation. I work alone."

Lucian shrugged and started to rise. "Then find the woman on your own. Or better, I will find her and catch Benito all by myself."

Hard determination glittered in Lucian's eyes. He'd do exactly what he said.

If Dane searched for Elena on his own, it could take months, maybe years, before he found her. He'd never beat Lucian in the race to find Elena. The only objective was to get Benito. And he'd sworn he'd do whatever it took to catch his sister's killer.

Like it or not, Dane needed Moss.

Dane leaned forward. "All right, I'll keep you in the loop."

"I want in on the *kill,* not the loop."

If he wanted Benito, he'd have to work with Lucian. "Agreed."

Lucian's shoulders relaxed and he sat back down. "It could take me a week or two to find her."

"How? She must move around a lot and live off the grid. There's been no trace of her."

Lucian didn't miss a beat. "Facial recognition scanner."

"Like the ones they use to track cheaters in Vegas?" Dane asked.

"Mine's a lot better. And unlike conventional technology mine is programmed to tap into every surveillance system in every major city. You can change your hair, put on glasses or a hat, but the bones in your face never change. If she's been through an airport, mall or bus station in the last nine months, I'll find her."

"You are certain?"

Lucian smiled. "Very."

Chapter 3

"Are you sure you're going to be okay if I leave you here for a few days?" Sheridan asked Kristen.

Kristen's smile was genuine. "I will be fine. Go to your sister." She had been working at the studio for two weeks and had fallen into a routine. She'd never felt more relaxed and confident.

"I hate leaving you." Sheridan frowned at the computer on the reception desk one last time. "The computer is no problem for you?"

"No." She'd picked up the Mac's system in a day.

"Computers are a necessary evil as far as I am concerned. But they are efficient and we've got new registrations to log in."

It felt good to be able to help Sheridan, who had done so much for her these last couple of weeks. Watching the studio for a few days and handling the computer was a pleasure. "I will do the computer work."

Silver bracelets jangled on Sheridan's wrist as she dragged her hand through tousled blond hair. "You are a goddess."

"Anything else?"

"If a girl named Crystal comes by looking for me, tell her I'll be back in a few days. She's one of the kids from the shelter. With a bit of work, I think I can save her."

"I'll keep a lookout for her." Kristen glanced at her dollar-store wristwatch. "You better go now or you'll be stuck in D.C. traffic."

Sheridan turned to leave and then snapped her fingers, as if remembering something. "We've also got that contractor coming." The plan was to convert the two small rooms off the reception area into a large tearoom.

"I remember. I can handle one contractor. Your sister is having a baby, Sheridan. Go to her."

Mention of the baby made Sheridan smile as she grabbed her large denim satchel. "You know it's a girl."

"Yes." She picked up Sheridan's suitcase and guided her out the front door. The fall air had turned cold over the past few days.

Sheridan glanced back at the studio one last time. "I don't know what I'd do without you, Kristen. My students love you. You're a wiz with this computer and a master with bookkeeping."

Kristen was the one who was grateful. These last two weeks had been the most peaceful she'd known in years. "Go."

Sheridan nodded, took her suitcase from Kristen and headed down the steps to a green VW Bug parked by the curb. Kristen stood on the front porch and waited as Sheridan started her car. However, instead of driving off, Sheridan shut the engine off and got out of the car.

Kristen shook her head, laughing. Sheridan was a brilliant teacher and her students loved her, but she was chronically late and could be scattered at times.

"I forgot to tell you about Simone Brady," Sheridan said.

Kristen laughed. "At the rate you are going that baby is going to be in college before you see her."

Sheridan smiled. "I promise this is the last thing. Simone is going to be calling."

Kristen came down the stairs and met her halfway. "For a class?"

"No, she's a reporter with the local paper and a stringer for the *Washington Post*. She's doing a piece on yoga studios in Virginia. She wants to do a story on us."

Kristen folded her arms over her chest. Publicity was great for Sheridan but the worst thing that could happen to her. Her voice sounded flat when she said, "Great."

Sheridan was so distracted about getting on the road that she didn't pick up on the shift in Kristen's voice. "She might call for background info before I return. Just tell her what she needs to know. When I get back, she'll be sending a photographer out."

Apprehension twisted the muscles in her back. "Why?"

Sheridan beamed. "She's going to take our picture."

Kristen drew in deep breaths, letting her rib cage expand as Sheridan had taught her. She'd taken great pains to disguise her appearance, but having her picture publicized was asking for trouble. Benito had contacts all over the country. She could never be in that picture. "You better get going."

Sheridan laughed. "Right." She got in her car and drove off.

Kristen retreated back into the house and closed the front door. She locked the deadbolt. The safety she'd felt behind these walls had vanished. Sheridan's mention of the photographer was a stark reminder that she could never be too careful. For the rest of her life she would need to look over her shoulder. Benito would never give up his search for her.

If Benito found her, he wouldn't kill her, but she'd already learned from him that there were worse things than death. Her heart began to race.

She raised a trembling hand to her forehead. Again, she drew in a calming breath. The more she breathed, the more her heart slowed.

There'd been no sign of Benito in nine months. She'd been very careful. She was okay. She was safe.

Kristen closed her eyes and turned away from the door. She tried to push the worries from her mind.

She would stay free of Benito.

She would be fine.

Heavy footsteps sounded on the front porch. She heard a knock. She opened her eyes and turned.

A very tall man with broad shoulders stood on the other side of the glass door. He wore faded jeans that draped muscular thighs, a worn gray Virginia Tech T-shirt and brown scuffed work boots. A Carolina Panthers ball cap shadowed his rawboned face.

She glanced at her watch. One-twenty. If this was her carpenter, he was early.

Her stomach tightened a notch. Reason tried to

rein in emotion. Surprises always made her nervous. She was far, far away from Benito and Sheridan had said a carpenter was coming.

Being ten minutes early didn't mean he was a trained killer. She studied the man. He pulled off his cap and smiled at her.

"I'm looking for Sheridan," he said through the glass. "I'm the carpenter."

She relaxed and moved to the door. She clicked back the latch. "Sorry," she said through the glass door. "You surprised me."

His expression changed to sheepish, almost boyish. "Sorry. I got a habit of showing up early when I go to a new job. I'd hate it if I got lost and was late for my first day on a job." His southern accent charmed her.

She opened the door. His thick black hair looked in need of a haircut. This close, she could see the sun-etched lines at the corners of very blue eyes. His nose had a ridge in the center, as if it had been broken. There was a ketchup stain on his shirt.

His deep, raspy voice had her pulse scrambling. And that was a surprise. She'd not looked twice at another man since Carlos.

"You must be Kristen Rodale," he said.

"How do you know my name?"

"Sheridan told me. She said she might have to go

out of town for a few days. Said a pretty blonde worked for her." He winked. "And I'm guessing that must be you."

She ran her hands through her short blond hair. "Right."

His suntanned hand was tucked casually in his pocket and his shoulders were relaxed. "Sorry again about startling you. I figured you must have heard my old truck pull up. The muffler is shot and makes a heck of a racket."

He seemed like a nice guy. And she was being overly paranoid. "I was lost in thought. Please come into the studio."

He chuckled, wiped his feet on the mat and came inside. "No worries. I zone out all the time."

She held out her hand. "I'm sorry, can you tell me your name again?" She knew the name but wanted to hear him say it first. Security always came first.

His large callused hand enveloped hers. Even white teeth flashed. "The name is Cambia. Dane Cambia."

Dane had used his real name. Something he hadn't done with the other leads Lucian had given him. Sloppy. Especially now, as Dane held Kristen Rodale's hand, he feared Lucian had gotten it wrong again. She looked nothing like Elena Benito.

This woman did not have Elena's long dark hair,

and the bleached-blond hair was a startling surprise. The short cut accentuated high cheekbones, pale skin and large brown, wary eyes.

Kristen wore loose-fitting black yoga pants that skimmed her calves. A snug electric-blue top hugged her full breasts. Like Elena, she wasn't tall—no more than five-one or -two—but she lacked Elena's curves. Kristen's body was lean. Her face was scrubbed clean of the heavy makeup Elena was so fond of and her nails weren't polished. She looked more like a teenager than a woman in her midtwenties.

Over the last two weeks, Dane had investigated three of the five identity hits Lucian's computer program had generated. When he'd seen the other women, one glance had told him they had the wrong woman. But to be thorough, he'd hung around each woman for a day, playing out the alias he'd fashioned for himself until Lucian could run the prints.

Now as he stood in the yoga studio, he thought about the time he'd waste today pretending to be a carpenter as he waited for an opportunity to get something with her prints on it. He never took shortcuts and he'd go through the motions, but already his mind was looking ahead to the next woman, in Kansas City, who Lucian had identified as a possible match.

"Mr. Cambia, welcome to the studio." Her voice was soft, hesitant, no hint of an accent.

"Thanks, ma'am."

She took a step back. "Sheridan said she gave you a tour yesterday."

"Yeah. I missed you." He'd been disappointed because he'd missed Kristen by seconds. In fact, he'd seen her walking down the street away from the studio. She'd been going to lunch and running errands for Sheridan.

"I usually get the middle of the day off." She didn't elaborate.

He smiled, projecting a relaxed appearance that was as fake as the accent. "Oh, no worries."

Kristen glanced toward the rooms Sheridan wanted renovated. "You know what needs to be done?"

"Oh, I sure do, ma'am. Sheridan told me."

She smiled and to his surprise his gut tightened a notch. Elena or not, this woman was a stunner. Her soft brown eyes reminded him that he'd been alone for a long time.

"Then I'll let you get to it. Let me know if you need anything."

He moved into the first room off the reception area. Like the one it connected to, this room was very small and unusable for anything more than storage. Sheridan wanted to knock out a wall between the rooms and turn the spaces into one large room. He flipped on the light.

Dane had done carpentry work with his foster father when he'd been a kid. The old man had made his living building houses and often took Dane and Nancy along to help.

"So have you been at the studio long?" He kept his voice even.

Kristen went behind the counter and turned on the computer. Beside the computer was a stack of blue forms that needed to be logged in. "Not that long."

He made a point of not looking directly at her when he spoke. A direct, assessing gaze signaled a predator for most women. "How do you like Lancaster Springs so far?"

"It's great."

Dane hated small talk, but it was necessary. "So Sheridan is about to be an aunt?"

The mention of the baby had her relaxing more. "Her sister went into labor early this morning. She's two weeks early. Sheridan had hoped to be here to supervise the project."

"Ah, my brother and his wife have five kids," he lied. "They are a wild bunch, but good kids. Every one is a joy. Does Sheridan's sister know if it's a boy or a girl?"

The remaining tension in her face faded. "Girl."

"They pick a name?"

"I didn't ask."

Now that was odd. Women usually asked about

that kind of stuff. Nancy always had. But it made sense. She didn't want to connect with anyone in case she had to take off soon.

He moved toward the desk. His six-foot-two frame loomed over her. Immediately, he sensed his height made her nervous, so he stepped back to allow her more space. It wouldn't do to spook her before he got a positive ID on her.

He glanced into the studio off the reception area. Soft recessed lights shone on thick carpet, a pile of rolled up mats and a stack of blankets. "So you into this yoga stuff?"

"I just started taking it from Sheridan."

He scratched his head. "I don't know a darn thing about yoga. But it seems a little odd to be stretching your body in every direction. For me a workout involves sweat."

She laughed at that. "There's more to it than you realize."

"You look like you could be a teacher. What do you need, a license?"

"Centeredness."

"What's that?"

She shrugged. "The ability to push the outside world from your mind and focus on one thing."

So she was distracted. Interesting. He shifted his gaze back to the room that would be reconstructed.

"So what are Sheridan's grand plans for this place after I've made it beautiful?" He knew he was supposed to be knocking down a wall, painting and building shelves.

"Sheridan wants to turn the room and the one connected to it into a tearoom slash boutique. She wants to be able to sell more yoga supplies—mats, clothes, chimes and eye pillows."

He leaned against the doorjamb. "Sounds like a smart business lady."

"She is."

He pulled a notepad from his back hip pocket. "Sheridan said there are no more classes until Monday and I can get started on demolition today. She also said you'd be sticking around in case I needed anything."

Again, the bright smile, which he sensed was genuine. "I'll be here."

He liked Kristen and he hoped she wasn't Elena. Once Elena realized why he'd come, she'd despise him.

"I could use a hand with the debris removal. It's not heavy work." He wanted to keep her close until Lucian made the ID. "I can pay ten bucks an hour."

Kristen's eyes widened at the extra-high wage. For an instant she looked tempted, and then she shook her head. "Thanks, but I work for Sheridan."

Loyal. That was very un-Elena. "So you stop and answer the phone when it rings. What else are you going to do this week?"

She glanced at the desk and the pile of unfolded flyers and empty envelopes. "I have brochures to get in the mail and registrations to enter."

"How long is that gonna take?"

She hesitated. "Four or five hours."

"You can do that in the evenings. Help me and earn some extra money."

She tapped her finger on the reception desk. "Doesn't that cut into your profits?"

Damn, but she was a cautious one. "The faster I get this job done, the better impression I make. I want Sheridan as a reference so I can build business in the area."

She folded her arms over her chest. "Your offer is very tempting—"

"I pay in cash at the end of each day," he said quickly before she could say no.

Her eyes brightened. Ah, there was the magic word—cash. She couldn't be pulling down much here. And if she were living on the run, she'd need all the cash she could scrape together.

"Okay."

Dane grinned. He held out his hand. "Then it's a deal?"

Reluctantly she took his hand. "It's a deal."

He held her hand an extra beat and then released it. "Great."

She pulled her hand free. "When do you want to get started?"

He shrugged. "No time like the present."

She nodded. "I'll just change."

"Perfect."

Without a word, he watched her dash up the back staircase.

Last night he'd been watching the place. He'd caught a glimpse of her trim body on the second floor before she'd closed the shades. Her living here would make her easier to monitor tonight. Easier to contain.

Today he'd get her fingerprints and give them to Lucian.

Tomorrow Lucian would confirm her ID.

He hoped she wasn't Elena Benito. Kristen Rodale struck him as a good person. And he didn't want to drag her into his dark world.

But if Kristen turned out to be Elena, he'd set aside whatever warm feelings he had.

He was going to catch Benito. No matter who he had to use.

Chapter 4

Kristen pulled on a pair of faded jeans and a white T-shirt. She neatly folded the yoga pants and top that Sheridan had given her and put both in her knapsack, which she always kept packed.

Her movements were deliberate, slow, a holdover from her days growing up with her brother. He hated disorganization and sloppiness and he'd expected her to be perfect. Her hand slid to her cheek as she remembered a time when he hit her so hard she'd have sworn her teeth had rattled in her head. He'd been angry that day because she'd left her shoes out in the middle of her bedroom. He'd tripped on them when he'd come into her room to wish her well in school. But the stinging red mark he'd left on her face had meant she couldn't go to school that day or the next. She'd been fifteen years old.

Kristen curled her fingers into a fist. Anger boiled inside her as she remembered how she'd cowered in front of him that day so long ago.

As she zipped the knapsack closed, she forced the memory from her mind and replaced it with Dane Cambia's quick smile. His deep voice swirled in her head. He'd said all the right things and seemed like one of the good guys. And she liked him.

Kristen put on her sneakers and went downstairs. She came into the reception area just as Cambia closed a flip phone and tucked it back in on his belt holster. Instinct had her tensing.

He heard her and turned. Even white teeth flashed. "That was fast. I was just on the phone with the hardware store. Wanted to make sure the lumber I ordered had arrived."

Feeling foolishly paranoid, she shoved her hands in her pockets. "Time is money, I suppose."

"You are right about that, Miss Kristen." He hitched his head toward the side door. "I've got my sledgehammer in the truck. The way I figure it, I'll knock down walls and you can drag debris to the construction Dumpster out back. I just checked, and see it's arrived."

"It came this morning."

"You mind helping me unload a few supplies from my truck? Many hands make light work."

She was glad to have something to do. "You're the boss."

He grinned before heading out the front door. She followed. When she reached the front stoop, she paused and looked from right to left. Her stomach knotted. She'd not had this sense of anxiousness in months and was surprised she felt it now. Dane stood by a white van, the back door open. The van gave her pause. She'd heard they were soundproof—the perfect place to put someone if you wanted to snatch them.

Dane had shifted his gaze from her to the van's interior. He started to pull out tools, totally relaxed.

What had gotten into her today?

She hurried down the stairs to the back of his van. Carpenter's tools filled the neatly organized interior—hammers on the right, nails in labeled drawers, saws hanging from hooks. But what caught her attention was the condition of the tools. They were well used: the hammers nicked, the drop cloths spattered with paint and the circular saw's handle worn. The wear and tear was tangible proof that Cambia was indeed a carpenter.

Her spirits lifting, she brushed bangs out of her eyes. "What would you like for me to carry?"

He handed her a drop cloth, eye protection and gloves as he hefted a large sledgehammer and crowbar out of the back. "This should be all we need to get started." He locked the back of the van and tucked his keys in his jeans pocket. "After you."

She headed back up the stairs, through the main door and into the small room. "So do we just tear the wall down?"

"I'll cut the electricity to the room and then start removing the drywall. After that I'll go for the studs and frame work."

His tall, broad form filled the doorway. It had been a long time since she'd looked at a man with desire. But unexpected warmth spread through her veins.

"What do you want me to do with this?" she asked, holding up the drop cloth.

He moved into the room past her to the wall that needed to be demolished. "Spread the cloth in the hallway to protect the hardwood floors. We'll contain the mess as much as we can."

"Right."

"Where's your fuse box, Kristen?"

"Basement. Far right corner."

"Great. Be right back. Might want to shut off the computer if it feeds into this circuit."

"Oh, yeah, right."

She quickly shut down the computer. Seconds later the lights in the reception area went out. The bright April sunshine shone through the large front window and provided enough light to see.

Cambia came back through the reception area and went to the room marked for demolition. Kristen followed. He shoved his large hands into well-worn gloves and started lightly tapping on the wall with his hammer. He looked confident and relaxed.

She enjoyed watching him work. "What are you doing?"

"Looking for the studs—the supporting wood under the drywall. As I knock on the wall I can tell by the sound if I'm close to one."

In the last nine months, she'd washed dishes, mucked out stalls, even tried to waitress, but she'd done nothing in construction and knew zero about it. "Oh."

She spread out the drop cloth, careful that it covered all the hardwood in the entry hallway. Sheridan had had the floors redone just a year ago and had been worried that Cambia would damage them.

He put on his safety glasses and tossed Kristen's to her. "Let's get rolling."

"Ready."

"You stand clear, Miss Kristen. A hunk of drywall might hit you and we want to keep you safe."

She stepped back. "Got it."

"When I give the okay you can start collecting debris. For now just wait."

"Okay."

He lifted the hammer over his head and smashed it into the wall. The resounding crack sounded like gunfire and made her jump.

Cambia turned. "That noise scare you?"

"No, no, I'm fine."

Who was she kidding? She would never be fine.

Cambia drove the sledgehammer, taking another hunk out of the wall. The energy of the strike reverberated through the hammer's wooden shaft up into his arms. Since Nancy's death, he'd been filled with pent-up rage and he'd wanted nothing more than to destroy everything in sight.

He remembered when his sister had first come to the foster home. He'd been thirteen, had lived in the home for two years and had fallen into a routine. Nancy had been ten years old. She'd had a broken arm and had been so afraid when she'd arrived. But instead of cowering, she'd given everybody, especially him, so much sass. At first he couldn't stand to be around her, but Mr. and Mrs. Bennett, who'd raised fifteen foster kids over the years, had been patient. In time, her anger had faded and she'd started to lighten up.

He'd found out later that Nancy's father had broken her arm. He'd been drunk and had hit her with his car when he'd zoomed out of their driveway. Eventually, the Bennetts got full custody.

Dane shoved out a breath. When Nancy had first died, he had played it by the book, going after Benito by conventional means. For months he'd waded through red tape as he'd tried to get to the monster. But he'd run into brick wall after brick wall and his frustration had grown steadily. A tremendous amount of effort and nothing to show for it.

But now, for the first time in a very long time he was doing something tangible. And it felt good. He hit the wall again and again. Within minutes an entire section had been stripped away. A sheen of sweat dampened his brow.

"So what did that wall do to you?" Kristen asked.

He took a moment to collect himself before he turned and faced her. She leaned on the doorjamb, her arms crossed under full breasts.

He wiped his gloved hand over his sweaty forehead. "Like you said, Kristen, time is money. The sooner I get this down the sooner you can start hauling debris out."

She studied him an extra beat as if she wasn't sure what to make of him.

He knew he had to lighten up, let go of the anger. He'd worked hard to make her relax around him. "Go ahead and put on those work gloves. I'll be ready for you in a minute."

Kristen nodded and pushed her hands into the gloves. "I'll get a broom."

"Sure."

When she disappeared, he moved to the door to make sure he hadn't scared her off. To his relief he heard her steps down the hallway as she returned.

He returned to hitting the wall. Soon, there was a pile of drywall that needed clearing and his arms ached.

When she reappeared with the broom, he said, "Have at it."

He wasn't quite sure what she'd do with the pile. By the looks of her she'd never done a day of manual labor in her life—Elena sure hadn't.

But without a word, Kristen started to collect the larger pieces in her arms. He picked up an armload himself and followed her out the back. Outside, she slid the side door of the battered red Dumpster and dumped her armload of fractured drywall inside it. Her once pristine shirt was covered in white drywall powder, as were her arms. However, without complaint she headed back inside for another load.

The two worked for the next hour, clearing out debris. When they'd removed most of the large pieces, he knocked more down. She carried more.

By four o'clock, they'd stripped the wall to its bones. And he could see that Kristen was tired. Her face was flushed, and sweat stained the front of her shirt.

"Let's take a break," he said.

She frowned. "But we aren't finished."

"The wall isn't going anywhere and I could use some water. You got a kitchen in this place?"

"In the back. Follow me."

As they moved up the center staircase of the shotgun-style row house, he noted she moved with her shoulders back, her hips swaying gently with each step. For the first time, he got a glimpse of the money and fine education Elena Benito had known.

Maybe she was the one.

"You move like a dancer," he said as they entered the small kitchen. Elena Benito had loved to dance. She took him to a small apartment furnished with a bed and kitchen table.

Her hand on the kitchen cabinet, she hesitated. "I don't dance."

He heard the hesitation in her voice. "Could have fooled me."

Long, delicate fingers wrapped around two white

mugs that read Yoga Studio. She turned on the tap, waited until the water was cool and then filled each mug. She handed him his, careful that their fingers did not brush. "We don't have glasses, just mugs, but they are clean."

"Works for me." He drank the water, amazed at how thirsty he'd become. "So what brings you to a place like this to work?" He noted the slight tension in her hands as they tightened around the mug.

"It's a job." She raised the mug to her lips and started to drink.

"Yeah, but what brought you to Lancaster Springs?"

She shrugged. "Lots of twists and turns, Mr. Cambia."

"You from Virginia?"

She lifted her gaze up to his. "You are a very curious man."

He grinned, mentally backing off. "You're pretty. Can't blame a guy for wanting to get to know you better."

A blush added color to her cheeks. "I have a boyfriend."

That caught him off guard. "Does he live around here?"

"Yes. You might meet him when he comes by to pick me up after work."

Kristen had become a practiced liar these last nine

months. Stories tripped off her tongue and sometimes she half believed them herself. Despite her attraction to Dane, it was best to keep him at arm's
length. Romance was a luxury she couldn't afford.

"What's his name?" Cambia refilled his cup at the
tap.

"Mark," she said easily. She'd used this made-up
boyfriend before.

"Mark," he said, testing the name. "What's he do?"

"He's a fireman." The trick was to keep the lies
simple so that the details didn't trip her up later. "Are
you ready to get back to work?" In truth, she hated
the idea of dragging more of that white board outside.
Her shoulders ached, as did her lower back. But the
work was preferable to the questions.

Cambia stared at her over the mug's rim as he
drained the last of the water. He set the mug down
in the sink next to hers. Then he seemed to change
his mind, picked up the mug again and refilled it
with water. "Let's call it a night. We've gotten a lot
done today."

"Sure." She couldn't wait to crawl into a hot
shower and let the warm water rush over her skin.

"Mind if I hold on to this mug?" He held it by the
handle. "I'm some kind of thirsty. I'll bring it back
in the morning."

"That's fine," she said.

"Sure." He allowed her to lead and he followed her down the narrow hallway to the reception area. He stayed a few feet behind her but his presence surrounded her. She was aware of each deliberate step, the thud of his boots and his earthy masculine scent. He had the aura of a hunter.

Dane Cambia might be a carpenter now, but he hadn't always been one.

He shoved his callused hands into his worn gloves. "So where are you and…what's his name?"

She didn't hesitate. "Mark."

"Right. Where are you going this evening?"

"I don't know. Dinner or a movie. We might stay in."

"You don't look like the type that would date a fireman."

"What do you mean?"

"You look like you'd hook up with a lawyer or a doctor. Some guy with enough scratch to take care of you right."

Carlos had been a doctor. "You make me sound shallow."

He shook his head. "Not at all. I just know quality, even when it's hauling out the trash."

Again, it struck her that he was playing some cat-and-mouse game with her. "Do you have something you want to say to me, Mr. Cambia? I don't appreciate your observations."

He shrugged as he moved to the front door, and paused. "I was just making conversation."

Kristen noted the powerful muscles under the old T-shirt. "You haven't always been a carpenter."

"No, I sure have not."

"What brought you here?"

He flashed a grin. "There's lots of construction in the northern Virginia area. It's a good place to earn a living."

The area was booming. Washington, D.C. residents were building weekend country homes to escape the rat race. "What did you do before you became a carpenter?"

He studied her. "I was in the army. Headed up a recon unit in the Middle East." He laughed. "But I wasn't good at it. Kept getting lost and I never was much good at taking orders. I'm good with my hands so figured I'd try carpentry."

Outside, a car door slammed. Kristen started. On reflex she looked out the side window at the house next door. It was the neighbor—Mrs. McKenzie.

"That your boyfriend?" he said.

"No."

"Right, he comes at five."

She changed the subject. "We made great progress today."

"Sure did."

An odd silence settled between them and she thought he'd offer her the money he owed her for today's work. However, he didn't. There'd been a time when she'd not have given it a second thought. Forty-five dollars was a small fortune now. "About my money…"

"Right." He carefully set the mug on the receptionist desk and then counted out the money and handed it to her. Their fingers brushed and her body tensed.

She quickly counted it again and shoved it in her pocket. "Thanks."

He picked up the mug by the handle. "So, I'll see you first thing in the morning."

"What time?"

"Seven too early? If we can get in a full day, then I've got a chance of finishing this job up a couple of days early."

"Sure, seven is good. I'm up early." *I'm up early.* The thought made her smile.

"Did I miss something?"

"No. It's just that when I was younger, my day never started before noon."

"So, did you work nights or were you just rich?"

Kristen realized her mistake. Her guard had slipped. Staying alive had meant keeping conversations about her to a minimum. "It doesn't matter."

"It does to me, but I won't press it. We all got a right to our privacy."

"Thanks."

He left through the front door and moved easily down the front steps. He climbed into his truck.

She closed and locked the front door.

Dane leaned out the open door of his van and poured the water out of the mug. Carefully, he lowered the mug into a plastic bag and zipped it closed. Soon he'd know if Kristen was Elena.

Chapter 5

After Dane left Kristen in the yoga studio, he pulled his van around the corner and parked in the municipal parking lot.

Lucian Moss, who was waiting for Dane in his blue pickup truck, got out and started toward the small coffee shop, as they'd agreed earlier. He wore a black AC/DC T-shirt. Moss went into the café and ordered a cup of coffee.

Cambia picked up Kristen's mug in the plastic bag and climbed out of his van. Glancing from left to right, he made sure no one was watching and then crossed the street and entered the shop. He ordered coffee and sat down across from Moss.

"You're late," Moss said.

Cambia glanced around the shop and then handed the mug to Lucian. "It couldn't be helped." He slid the Baggie across the table.

Moss tucked the mug in his bag. "So what is she like?"

Cambia sipped his coffee. "The last thing I expected."

Moss's gaze sharpened. "Do you think we have the wrong one?"

Dane considered the question. There were only hints of the princess who'd spent most of her twenty-five years on the Miami beaches and in exclusive clubs. But it was her. "No."

"Excellent."

"She's very different."

"Nine months on the run can change anybody."

Dane had a sense of what she'd endured on the streets, but couldn't imagine how she'd dealt with it. "Once you've run the prints and we have a confirmation, then we'll move forward."

"Why not start now?" Moss's gaze was lean and hungry.

Knowing they'd found Elena should have made Dane happy—did make him happy. When they caught Benito they'd not only dispose of a cold-blooded killer, but they'd put a major dent in the south Florida drug-trafficking trade.

Despite all that could be gained, a part of him was also very sorry. He liked "Kristen." To his surprise, *she'd* gotten under his skin. "I want to be sure. Only then do we set the trap."

Chapter 6

Thursday, May 17, 6:55 a.m.

Since her escape from the safe house, it had become Kristen's habit to rise before the sun. In her old life, she'd only seen the sunrise when she'd been coming home from a club or party. Then dawn's red glowing rays signaled an ending. Now, it represented new beginnings.

She sat in the half-lotus position on her yoga mat in the center of Sheridan's studio. The lights were dim and she'd put on a calming CD. In the beginning, she felt a little silly sitting here like this, but Sheridan had insisted it would help her focus and concentrate.

Her work with Cambia yesterday had left her body stiff, and her muscles ached. But the discomfort didn't bother her. As hard as life had been this last year, there was satisfaction. Despite all odds, she was surviving, even prevailing.

Kristen turned to the right, gently twisting the tightness from her back. She closed her eyes and tried to clear her mind.

But instead, the sense of well-being faded. Dark thoughts from the past crept into her mind. She tried to push them aside but they grew stronger, pulling her back to the past.

Sitting in the limo's plush interior across from her brother, Elena clenched her hands in tight fists. Tinted windows prevented her from seeing outside. But judging by the roughness of the road, the car had turned off the main highway onto a side street.

Antonio had insisted she dress tonight in something bright and cheerful. Instead, she'd chosen a severe black dress which, combined with her long black hair, made her look pale.

The scent of Antonio's aftershave blended with the smoke of his Cuban cigar. He wore a white hand-made suit that fit his muscular frame perfectly. Gold links winked from white linen cuffs. His dark hair, peppered with gray at the temples, was slicked back. "I'm not happy with you, Elena. That dress is unsuitable."

His soft accent didn't disguise the steel beneath the words.

Elena did not care what Antonio thought anymore. She wore black because she was in mourning for the man she'd loved and lost. "You were responsible for the car accident that killed Carlos."

He puffed on his cigar and stared at her through the trail of smoke curling around his face. "He was not suitable."

To have her fears confirmed made her sick. "So you did kill him?"

"Yes."

"My God," she whispered.

Antonio had forbidden her to see Carlos, which had only solidified her determination to see him. A week ago she and Carlos had planned to run away. A day later his car had plunged off a bridge and he'd been killed.

"In time you will thank me," he said. "You are above the rest of the world. You are special. Your place is at my side and when the time is right I will choose a husband for you."

Unshed tears burned the back of her throat, but she refused to let them spill.

As if on cue, the car stopped. "Time for our lesson."

Elena could feel her resolve fraying. "Where are we?"

The door to the limo opened. Antonio got out and then held his hand out to her. His manicured nails caught the moonlight.

Elena didn't accept his hand but climbed out of the car unassisted. Anger glimmered in Antonio's dark eyes but he let the small act of defiance go.

Elena looked around and realized they were in the warehouse district. Before them stood three of Antonio's muscled men standing in front of a gray tobacco warehouse. They wore white linen suits, bright shirts and gun holsters they made no move to hide.

Elena had suspected Antonio was a criminal since she was a teenager, but he'd always kept that part of his life separate from her.

He guided her to the open warehouse door. She was aware only of the pounding of her heart and the click of her heels against the damp concrete.

The instant they entered the warehouse, she saw the six men. They kneeled in a neat row, hands tied behind their back. Their weathered faces bruised and tight with fear.

Antonio snapped his fingers and one of the men handed him a gun. He looked at her, his eyes cold

*and black. "These men disobeyed me, Elena. And
now you will see what happens to people who defy
me."*

Antonio fired his gun and killed the first man.

Kristen jumped, realizing the loud sound she'd
heard wasn't gunfire from the past. Someone was
pounding on her front door.

She glanced up at the clock hanging on the wall
across from her. Six-ten. Cambia would not be here
for at least another hour. No one should be here.

Her heart hammering, she rose and moved bare-
footed to the front door. A fine sheen of sweat
dampened her back and she realized her hands were
shaking. She shoved out a breath and tried to calm her
thoughts.

Thick blinds covered the glass front door, making
it impossible for her to see who was on the other side.
Instinct told her not to answer.

The someone on the other side pounded harder.
"Hey, Sheridan, it's me, Crystal. Let me in."

Crystal. The young girl Sheridan head mentioned.

"Come on, Sheridan, I can hear your yoga tape in
there. Please open up. Tony is coming." Desperation
dripped from the last word.

Kristen peeked around the edge of the curtain. A
girl stood there. Shoulder-length black hair accen-

tuated thickly made-up green eyes. She sported three earrings in each ear and a purple bruise on her cheek.

Kristen smoothed a damp hand down her yoga pants. Crystal was clearly in trouble. There'd been so many times when she'd wished someone would have reached out a hand and saved her.

Drawing in a deep breath, she turned the deadbolt and opened the door until the chain caught.

Crystal's gaze locked with Kristen's. "Please, lady, let me in."

In the distance she heard a squeal of wheels on pavement. Seconds later a red Cutlass Supreme came around the corner.

Crystal's face turned pale. "He's here."

Kristen watched as the car skidded to a stop in front of the building. In the front seat she could see a young man with tattoos on his neck and arms glaring at Crystal.

"Please, lady, please," Crystal begged.

Kristen unhooked the chain, grabbed the girl by the arm and pulled her in just as Tony bounded up the stairs to the studio.

Kristen shoved the door closed only to have Tony block it with his booted foot. He wrapped his ringed fingers around the door and began to shove against it. Kristen could feel Crystal clinging to her and she struggled to keep the door closed. But Tony was stronger than her. He pushed the door open.

Kristen, with Crystal behind her, stumbled back. She regained her footing, planted her feet on the ground and blocked his path to Crystal.

Kristen's memory flashed to a time when Antonio had lost his temper with her. He'd knocked her to the ground. She'd been too afraid to fight back. She had let her brother rule her life for too long. She'd had it with bullies. Tony would not hurt his girl.

Kristen faced Tony. "Get out of my house."

Tony sneered as if she amused him. "Give me Crystal and I'll leave."

The girl whimpered behind her. Kristen's own fear made her sick to her stomach but she refused to back down. "You can't have her."

Tony bared his teeth. The right incisor was capped in gold. "I can beat the crap out of you, too. Makes no difference to me."

She lifted her chin. "I won't make it easy for you."

He drew back his fist and landed a blow to Kristen's stomach. She dropped to her knees as Crystal backed away. Instinct had her curling her fingers into a fist. She might not be able to inflict much damage on Tony but she wouldn't be a pushover. She would fight him.

To her surprise, she heard Tony yelp.

She opened her eyes to see Dane Cambia standing behind Tony. He'd wrapped his muscled arm with expert efficiency around the punk's neck and had forced him to the ground. Tony's face was contorted with pain and anger.

"Let go of me, you bastard," Tony said.

Cambia tightened his hold, shoving his forearm into Tony's windpipe. "Give me one reason why I shouldn't just break your neck right now."

The raw anger in Cambia's voice belied the easy manner he'd exuded yesterday.

Kristen pulled in a painful breath, testing to make sure her ribs weren't broken.

"Are you all right?" Cambia demanded.

"Better." She straightened her torso and drew in another breath. The pain was easing.

Cambia's gaze flickered to her. Seeing her seemed to make him angrier. He wrenched Tony's army behind his back again.

Crystal wiped her nose with the back of her hand. "How does it feel now, Tony?" Despite her brave words she stood squarely behind Kristen.

"I'm gonna kill you!" Tony said to Crystal.

Cambia choked off the hood's breath again. "Provided you live that long."

The violence turned Kristen's stomach. "Don't," she wheezed. She struggled to her feet.

"Let the police take care of him," Crystal said.

Tony lurched toward her. Dane jerked him back. "I don't need the police to take care of him."

Fear registered in the punk's face when he stared at Dane.

Kristen had to agree with Dane. Police involvement was the last thing she wanted. Antonio had his fingers in too many police departments and if Tony were arrested, she'd have to file a complaint. Her alias would end up in computer files. She couldn't do that.

"Just get him out of here," Kristen said.

Tony grinned.

Dane grabbed a handful of the thugs's hair and jerked his head back. "If I see you around here again, I will make you very sorry."

Fear again darkened Tony's eyes. "Fine."

Cambia let him go, giving him a shove toward the curb. He watched, his hands on his hips like a brawler, as Tony hurried toward his car. He looked back at Crystal. "This ain't over between us."

Crystal jutted out her chin, all bravado. "We're done, Tony."

He climbed in his car and revved the engine. "Not by a long shot."

As he pulled away, his tires screeching on the pavement, Kristen raised trembling fingers to her forehead. The violent encounter reinforced memories of the murders of the Churchmen and Nancy. Her knees felt week.

"This isn't over," Cambia said. He faced her. "He will be back."

"His kind always come back," she said.

Dane held her gaze. "I will be here to protect you."

But for how long? If Kristen had learned anything this last year it was that she was alone in this world and couldn't depend on anyone.

Crystal sniffed. "Why didn't you just call the cops?"

Dane faced her. "He'd be back on the streets in a day or two."

Crystal nodded. "Yeah. Well, it's been real, but I better get going." Her hand on her backpack, she started past Cambia.

His arm shot out and he grabbed her. "Why'd you come here?"

She tried to wrestle her arm free but couldn't. "Sheridan is my friend. We met at the youth center. She said if I had trouble to find her."

"What does Tony want with you?"

Cheap silver bracelets jangled on her wrist as she dug her fingers through her dirty hair. "He's mad at me."

"What did you do? And don't B.S. me," Cambia said.

She shrugged. "I told him not to hide his drug stash at the youth center but he wouldn't take me seriously. One of the younger kids found it and would have swallowed it if I hadn't caught him. So I flushed it."

Cambia's jaw tightened then released. "Crystal, stay away from Tony."

Mascara stained the delicate skin under her eyes. "Oh, don't you worry. I want no part of him."

Kristen hoped Crystal meant what she said. She'd watched Antonio's girlfriends take all sorts of abuse only to return to him as if nothing had happened.

"Mr. Cambia, let her go," Kristen said.

Cambia released Crystal. The girl quickly hurried down the steps and across the street. She didn't look back.

Kristen straightened, wincing as her bruised ribs shifted. "Some morning."

Cambia locked the front door. His gaze shifted to her midsection. "Did he hurt you badly?"

"Just knocked the wind out of me."

Tension radiated from his body. "Let's get you inside. You could have a broken rib."

"My ribs are fine. I just need to change and we can get started working." When she moved she winced.

Cambia shook his head. "First you sit and drink a coffee or tea. I want to make sure for myself that you are okay before you do any lifting today."

It was tempting to let him baby her, but the truth was she felt better keeping her distance. "I can take care of myself."

Irritated, he shoved fingers through his hair. "Yeah, well, right now you don't have to. Let's go to the kitchen."

She suspected moving a mountain would have been easier than changing his mind right now. "Fine."

He followed up the stairs to her small apartment. By the time she reached the small kitchen table, her right side ached.

"Sit," he ordered.

Grateful, she sat at the small table. "Sheridan has coffee stocked in the shelves. I usually drink tea."

He brushed her aside. "I'll make tea."

"I'm out. I'd planned to pick some up at the market last night, but forgot." The truth was the green tea she liked wasn't on sale and at $3.99 a box it was a luxury she couldn't afford right now.

"Fine. Coffee then."

As she drew in a careful breath, she studied the deep frown lines on his face. "Where's the easygoing guy from yesterday?"

Her comment caught him off guard. With an effort, he shrugged, but tension remained in his body. "I don't like men that hit women."

Dane had saved her and she was arguing with him.

She'd been on her own so much she'd forgotten how to take help. "I'm sorry. I should be thanking you."

"No problem." Cambia put grounds in the top of the pot, poured the water in and flicked on the switch. Quickly, the coffeemaker began to gurgle and spit. Cambia's presence dominated the room, which now seemed too small.

"I don't have milk or sugar." More luxuries that she'd decided she could live without.

"Black's fine."

Having him wait on her felt awkward so she rose and from the cabinet, got down two white mugs that said Yoga Studio on them. Stretching made her wince.

"So you *are* hurt," Cambia said.

She set the mugs down, breathing through the pain. "Just a little sore."

He stepped toward her. "I'm taking you to the doctor."

"I don't like doctors."

"You could have broken ribs." He nodded toward her loose-fitting yoga blouse. "Let me see your ribs."

"Not likely, Cambia." The idea of his hands touching her made her more nervous than she thought possible.

He lifted a brow. "It's either me or the doctor."

Kristen didn't want to press him. She had no doubt he'd drag her to the doctor if need be. Again, she'd end up in somebody's computer system. "No doctors." She faced him. "Okay, check."

He pressed his large hands to her rib cage under her loose top. Her pulse quickened. But she didn't dare move for fear his hands would touch the underside of her breasts.

His hands stretched wide, nearly reaching around the circumferance of her chest. However, his movements were all business and very gentle.

She winced as he squeezed softly. "That hurts."

"Yes." His chin grazed the top of her head. She was very aware of his scent, a mixture of soap and his own aroma.

His thumb brushed the underside of her breast and a thousand tiny bolts of energy shot through her body. She tried to step back but bumped into the counter.

"Stop squirming," he said.

Unwanted desire warmed her body. "Look, I'm fine."

He held on to her a second longer, then released her. "I don't think anything's broken but you're going to be sore for a couple of weeks. Bruises can take longer to heal than breaks."

Her breathing had grown shallow. It had been almost a year since she'd been with a man. Carlos, her fiancé, had been the only man she'd ever bedded.

After he'd died, she hadn't had the desire or the energy for another man. While she'd been on the run, there'd been opportunities for sex, but she hadn't trusted anyone enough to take the risk.

Now, however, she was very aware of her enforced celibacy. She moistened her lips.

Cambia's eyes darkened as he stared down at her lips.

Slowly, as if she were a skittish colt, he raised his hand to her elbow. His callused hands felt rough against her skin. Gently, he traced circles on her forearm with his thumb.

Her mouth felt dry and her heart started to pound against her ribs. All she had to do was lean forward an inch or two and her breasts would rub against the faded blue T-shirt that stretched across his chest.

So dangerous. So very dangerous.

Yet, the pull was more than she could deny. She'd been alone for so long and she wanted to feel connected to someone, if only for a short while.

Sensing the first move would have to be hers, she rose up on her tiptoes and gently kissed his lips. At first, he stood as rigid as a statue, staring down at her as if he were seeing her for the first time.

She kissed his lips a second time, fearing she'd misjudged him and she was offering something that he didn't want.

However, the second kiss was all the encouragement he needed. He banded his arm around her and gently pulled her to him, deepening the kiss. His tongue parted her lips and began to explore.

She relaxed into the kiss, wrapping her arms around his neck. Pain forgotten, her body started to hum and her nerves danced. Raw need pulsed in her veins. She'd known this man less than a day. He was a stranger. A very dangerous stranger.

Yet, emotion and desire overruled reason. Kristen needed to feel like a woman who enjoyed her sexuality. She was so tired of being the hunted, frightened creature.

Cambia's hand slid down her waist to her buttocks. He squeezed her bottom. The thin yoga pants were little barrier to his touch and she felt as if she were naked.

He pressed her hips forward until her body pressed against his erection. The bed was only three feet away and there was no doubt now that they would be in it within seconds.

Cambia nipped her ear with his white teeth. She slid her hands under his T-shirt and up his muscled chest. He felt so good, so alive.

Kissing her again, he started to step back toward the bed, tugging her with him. She followed and reached for the thick belt buckle at his narrow waist.

When her knuckles brushed his bare skin, he drew in a breath as if he'd exploded right then and there.

Kristen reveled in her womanly power. It felt so good to be in control and know what she wanted even for this very brief time.

She unhooked his belt and unfastened his pants. Her hand slid down toward his erection. He moaned. Without warning, his cell phone rang on his belt holster.

The loud sound startled her. But her desire still burned hot.

With great effort, Cambia released her. His breathing was ragged, as if he'd just run a dozen miles. "I've got to get it."

"They can leave a message." Her voice sounded unrecognizable but she didn't care. Selfishly, she wanted this moment because she felt so wonderfully alive. And to think it wouldn't happen now was beyond her circle of reasoning.

The phone rang again, louder and more insistent.

Cambia muttered an oath and fumbled for the phone. He flipped it open. "Cambia."

Frowning, he turned his back to her.

The gesture felt like a rejection. And immediately, Kristen's desire evaporated. Her mind cleared. She shoved trembling hands through her hair. Good Lord, what had she been thinking? She'd been ready to make love to this man right here.

She had not only thrown herself at a virtual stranger, but she'd given no thought to the consequences. What if she'd gotten pregnant?

Fool.

A moment's fun could easily have landed her with more problems than she needed.

It wasn't like her to lose control.

Cambia's shoulders tensed. "You're absolutely sure?" He hesitated, listening. "Fine."

He closed the phone and replaced it carefully in its holster.

Drawing in a deep breath, Dane faced her. The desire had vanished from his face.

In its place was a coldness that made her tremble.

Chapter 7

Facts now confirmed what Dane had known in his gut. The prints were a perfect match. Kristen Rodale *was* Elena Benito.

And Dane had nearly made love to her. Another minute and he'd have been inside her.

Damn. All the time and energy he and Lucian had put into finding her and he'd nearly jeopardized the entire operation. He'd acted like a teenager with more hormones than brains.

He needed to keep his distance from her. She wasn't a woman to be desired or loved. She was business. Nothing more than bait to trap the animal Antonio Benito.

Single-minded focus on the objective had made him one of the best in the army recon unit and the bureau. And the objective in this operation was capturing Antonio Benito. No matter what the cost.

He cleared his throat, noticing the dark roots of Kristen's hair. In his case-file pictures, she'd had long, lush black hair, and he wondered when she'd cut and dyed it blond. The hair change had completely transformed her appearance. It accentuated the high slash of her cheekbones and made her beautiful eyes stunning. It gave Kristen an air of directness Elena had not possessed.

Damn. It didn't matter if the package wrapping had changed. This woman was Elena Benito. She was the bait. And nothing else.

Dane needed to diffuse the energy between them. "I'm sorry. I shouldn't have let things get away from me."

Her cheeks turned a delicate red, but she held his gaze like the proud princess she was. "I shouldn't have kissed you."

He shoved his hand in his pocket, wishing she didn't still look so desirable. "Let's just chalk this up to bad judgment."

For a moment he thought sadness flickered in her

eyes but it was gone as quickly as it had come. "Sounds good."

She nodded toward the coffeemaker. "You still want that coffee?"

A cold shower would have been better. "Yeah, sure."

Kristen poured a cup and handed it to him, careful not to touch him. Whatever had happened between them had surprised her, as well. Good. He wasn't the only one off balance.

"Thanks," he said, taking the cup.

She turned to pour herself a mug. "Something puzzles me."

The cup to his lips, he hesitated. "What's that?"

A wrinkle furrowed her smooth forehead. "What were you doing here this morning?"

The tension in her voice sharpened his senses. "We had an appointment."

The worry in her eyes remained. "For seven o'clock. Not six."

He grinned. Charming, not defensive. "I am a little compulsive about time. I was hoping if I showed up early I could get a jump on the project."

The truth was he'd been outside all night. After he'd met with Lucian, he'd returned and parked down the block from her house. With cash in her pocket, he worried that she'd slip away.

His explanation seemed to satisfy her somewhat,

but not completely. "You'd have sat outside for an hour waiting if I hadn't answered."

He shrugged. "It was a risk."

She studied him as if trying to put the pieces of the Dane Cambia puzzle together. "You must really want the work."

"You've got to have a little skin in the game if you want to build your name."

"Right." She drew out the word, telegraphing her uncertainty.

He set down his cup. Questions only stirred trouble. "I better start unloading. Come down when you've finished your coffee."

"I'm finished. I can help you."

"No heavy lifting today."

She didn't argue, a sign that her ribs still hurt. He thought about that punk hitting her. Swift hot rage sliced through him.

They headed down the hallway to the front reception area. "Why don't you wait inside?" he said. "I'll be back in a minute with the supplies."

"Sure."

She stood inside the studio as he went out to his truck, stopping and glancing from left to right. Benito, Tony, there was no telling who was going to crawl out of the woodwork.

Benito would arrive soon enough, but Dane suspected Tony wasn't likely to come back while he was here. The punk would wait until Kristen was alone to take his revenge.

A satisfied smile tipped the edge of his lips when he remembered the fear in Tony's eyes. What the punk didn't get was that she had his protection now. Tony would never get a second chance to hurt her.

Dane unloaded his sledgehammer and then moved around the side of the van, out of Kristen's line of sight. He set down the tool and snapped his cell phone out of its belt holster. He flipped it open and dialed Lucian.

The phone rang once before Moss answered. "Yep."

"So give me the details." He turned his back to the house, still scanning the streets for trouble.

"Like I said earlier, the prints are a perfect match. Little Miss Yoga is Elena Benito."

"There's no mistaking the results?" The edge of hope in his voice surprised him.

"I don't make mistakes." Lucian sounded offended.

"Good." He shoved his hand through his hair. Like it or not he had a mission to finish. "So we move forward."

"I'll start leaking news that Elena Benito is living in Virginia. It won't take more than a couple of days for the information to filter through Benito's organization before word reaches him."

"Let me handle that. I've got a source that could be helpful on this one."

He hesitated. "Okay."

"And in the meantime I babysit."

"She is the golden goose. Without her we have nothing to bait the trap with."

"Right."

Lucian hesitated. "You sound different. Is something wrong?"

He squinted as he looked toward the morning sun. "What do you mean?"

"Like you're having second thoughts."

"No doubts."

"Good. Because I am going to catch Benito with or without your help."

Resentment surged through him. "I don't need a lecture. I know my job." Before Lucian could reply, Dane added, "I do need for you to do something."

"Yes?"

"There's a punk in this neighborhood named Tony. Early twenties. I don't have a last name for him but ask around and you can find it."

"I can do that."

"This guy must have a rap sheet. See if he has any outstanding warrants. I need him in jail until this is over. He could cause problems we don't need."

"Consider it done."

"Good." He hung up, shoved the cell back in its belt holster and picked up his equipment. As he climbed the front stairs, he caught a glimpse of Kristen in the front window.

She reminded him of the fabled sirens—beauties who lured sailors to their deaths. He couldn't help but wonder if she was as dangerous as the sirens. Yes, she appeared vulnerable and kind. But her brother was a skilled chameleon. Benito could be charming and giving. He'd seduced the Miami social world with elegant parties that included all A-list people and huge donations to the right charities.

He tightened his hold on the toolbox. Whether her heart was pure or as black as Satan's, he would stay objective.

He owed that much to Nancy.

Kristen joined Dane in the room under construction. He stood by the large window. He wore a clean T-shirt but had on his same grungy pair of jeans and boots. From his narrow waist hung his tool belt, cocked at an angle like a fabled gunslinger's belt.

She glanced at his long hands resting on his hips. Her pulse quickened when she thought about them on her body.

Kristen straightened. She couldn't think this way about him. It wasn't safe for anyone to care about her.

She flexed swollen and tired fingers, a reminder of her hard labors yesterday. "Last night it was difficult to judge the progress but this morning with the sunlight streaming in, I can see that Sheridan had been right to knock down the wall."

Dane glanced at the skeletal frame and the exposed wires running between the two-by-fours. "By the end of today this will all be gone and you will really start to see it come together. Yesterday was a good first day."

First day. These past months had been a study in firsts. First haircut and dye job. First bus ride. First night sleeping in a doorway. Her first paycheck.

"So where do you want me to start?" she said, walking into the room.

He turned as she approached. "I'll take the wires out and then we knock down the wood. For now just take it easy."

"You're paying me to help."

"You'll get your chance soon enough. For now, relax."

Relaxation was tough for her. It gave her too much time to think. "Sure."

"I've got to turn off the electricity again." He'd turned the breakers back on last night in case she needed to use the computer. "Computer off?"

"I finished the entries last night. Everything is saved and it's off."

"You worked more last night? What about Mark?"

"Had to work late."

"Ah."

He studied her an extra beat. "I'll just head to the basement and flip those breakers."

She followed him to a small door that took them down rickety steps to a dank basement. Sheridan had given her the grand tour so she knew the light switch was at the top of the stairs. She flipped up the old switch.

A single light bulb hanging from a wire clicked on. It cast an eerie circle of light on the blackened room. She didn't venture off the step.

He moved past her and down the stairs. "You don't like the basement." He opened the tiny metal door, studied the circular fuses and unscrewed the one controlling the upstairs room.

She shuddered dramatically. "Utter blackness, creepy spiders and rats. What's not to love?"

He grinned. "Darkness never hurt anybody and chances are the little beasties that live down here are more afraid of you than you are of them."

She heard something scurry in the corner and cringed. "That's up for debate."

"You're such a girl," he teased.

That comment made her laugh as she backed up the stairs. "And proud that I can't throw a baseball or change a tire."

When he reached the top he closed the cellar door. "What if you had to go down there and change a fuse?"

"I didn't say I couldn't deal with the things in the basement. I would if I had to. But the less monsters in my life the better."

He studied her, his gaze razor sharp. "Are there monsters in your life?"

Her heartbeat quickened. Despite the casual tone, his question hit a nerve. Since her parents had died ten years ago, all she'd had in her life were monsters. "I suppose we all have monsters."

"I suppose you're right."

He moved back toward the front of the house, to the room under construction. She trailed behind him. He turned the light switch, and when he confirmed the juice was not flowing, he pulled out a pair of wire cutters. "So who are your monsters, Kristen?"

Fear scraped her nerves. She folded her arms over her chest, feigning a bravery she didn't have. "My father always taught me never to talk about them. Talking stirs fear and fear feeds the monsters."

He clipped a white wire in tow. "So where is your mother?"

Questions normally put her on the defensive. But

for some reason, with Dane she wasn't afraid to answer. "My mother and father died in a car accident."

"I'm sorry." He kept his gaze on his work but she sensed he was keenly aware of her. "When did they die?"

The old pain of her parents' death had lessened from agony to a dull throb, but it was always present. "Ten years ago."

"Sorry to hear that. How old were you?"

Kristen hugged her arms around her chest. "I was fifteen."

She'd barely spoken about her mother or father in years. Antonio had forbidden her to. He'd never forgiven his father for marrying Kristen's Anglo mother after his own mother's death. Antonio's mother, from what he'd said, had been a quiet superstitious woman who was content to dote on her son. Kristen's mother had been a tall, blond actress who liked to spend money and throw lavish parties. Antonio had resented his father and his second wife. He'd been thirty when they'd died in the car crash, and had taken over his father's fortune and brought Kristen to live with him.

Dane glanced over his shoulder at her. "That's rough."

"It was a bad time for me." Her voice shook only a little when she spoke.

"So where'd you go?"

She didn't even like thinking about the years spent living in her brother's house, let alone talking about them. "I went into foster care." She'd used the lie often this last year. The fewer people who knew the truth about her the better.

"Was foster care rough?"

"Not really," she lied. "The people who took me in were kind and loving. They kept me until I turned eighteen."

His jaw tightened then released. "You keep up with them?"

"Sure. I write whenever I get the chance."

Dane clipped another end of the white thick wire and sealed off the end. "Looks like we have more in common than I realized."

"How's that?"

"I grew up in foster care."

"You did?" What she knew about foster care came from television shows and books. She needed to choose her words carefully. "Did your parents die?"

"Naw. They're still out there somewhere alive and well. They just couldn't tackle the work it took to raise a kid. My old man couldn't hold down a job and my mother drank."

"I'm sorry." At least she'd known her parents had loved her. "Did you have a brother or sister?"

With a violent yank, he pulled the white wire though the holes it had been threaded through in the wood. He didn't look at her but she could see the tension in his shoulders. "A foster sister."

"You two close?"

"We were."

"Were?"

"She died about nine months ago."

"I'm sorry," she said softly. "What happened?" The question felt rude but had slipped out before she could stop it.

He faced her, his expression a mixture of sadness and anger. For a moment, she didn't think that he would answer. "She was a cop. She was shot and killed in the line of duty."

A hard jolt rocked her body. Sudden, violent memories of that last night in the Miami safe house slammed into her. She remembered the shots fired, the shouts and the order from Nancy Rogers to run. And God help her, like a coward she had run.

Not a day went by that she didn't think of Nancy. She thought about the policewoman's family. Wondered if she'd left children and family behind.

"You all right?" Dane's voice sliced through her grief.

She swallowed unshed tears and lifted her chin. Sloppy emotion wasn't going to bring anyone back. "Yes, I'm fine." She sniffed and managed the bright smile she used when her brother expected her to be happy. "My goodness, how did we get on such dark topics?"

He turned back to his work. "The darkness is in all of us. And sometimes it slips out when we least expect it."

The smile faded. "I feel surrounded by darkness. And it's only the light that breaks through on occasion for me."

Dane ripped the last of the wire out and started to wind it around his arm. "What do you say we have dinner tonight?"

The sudden shift threw her off balance. "Dinner? What brought that on?"

"Maybe we should let a little light in through the dark. It would do us both good to have a little fun."

His offer tempted far too much. But she'd already proven that she had a weakness for him. "I don't think so."

Dane lifted a brow. The sadness had vanished and in its place was challenge. "You got something better going on with that boyfriend of yours?"

"No, Mark is working again tonight. I promised Sheridan I'd wash the wool yoga blankets."

"So you'd prefer wet blankets over me?"

A smile tipped the edge of her lips. "You make it sound awful. I didn't mean it that way."

Amusement danced in his eyes. "I've been ditched before, but never for wet blankets."

The sadness squeezing her heart lifted. "Fine. I'll have dinner with you."

He shook his head, feigning irritation. "Hey, don't do me any favors, lady. I am not that hard up for a night out."

Dane's southern accent deepened, softening his words even more. She laughed. And Lord, but it felt good. "I'd like to have dinner with you."

He nodded, clearly satisfied. "It's a date."

Chapter 8

Cambia finished his work for the day at the studio and drove to his motel room. Instead of getting out of the van, he sat very still for a moment. Tinted windows blocked what remained of the afternoon sun. He opened the disposable and untraceable cell phone he'd bought before he came to town. Instead of dialing, he hesitated. He dreaded what had to be done next.

The day with Kristen had gone well. There'd been no more kisses. In fact, she had been careful not to touch him. But she'd made him a lunch of peanut butter and jelly sandwiches and potato chips. She'd insisted on working if he was going to pay her so he'd given her small pieces of lumber to take to the Dumpster. She'd done the work without complaint and as the hours ticked by she'd grown more relaxed.

He was winning her trust.

And now he was going to betray her.

The idea bothered him. Far too much.

Dane flipped down his sun visor. Attached was a strip of pictures taken of Nancy and him a few years ago in one of those photo booths at the state fair. The pictures had been her idea and he'd only gone along begrudgingly. In the first shot they'd tried to be serious but by the last shot she was making a face and he was laughing.

He touched the strip of pictures. Nancy had come up to Montana and he'd convinced her to go to the fair. She dubbed it all back-country nonsense, but by the end of the night, after she'd ridden the Ferris wheel, eaten two cotton candies and won a stuffed dog at the balloon toss, she'd admitted they'd had a blast.

It was the last real fun they'd had together. They had sworn they'd get together soon. But *soon* had turned into months and years. Until finally, they'd run out of time.

He thought about that last cell phone call from the safe house. He thought about the moment he'd handed the folded flag at her funeral to her fiancé, a large hulking man who'd openly wept.

Anger flooded Dane's body, recharging his resolve. For Nancy's sake, he would stay the course.

He dialed the number of a bar called Maria's down in Miami. The place was frequented by drug dealers and served as a makeshift message center. He'd been monitoring the place for quite some time.

The phone rang. On the fifth ring, he heard a gruff, "Maria's."

"Get me Ortiz," Dane said. Manuel Ortiz was Benito's eyes and ears in the bar. "I got news on the king's sister." The king was Benito.

Wariness mingled with anticipation. "What kind of news?"

"I only talk to Ortiz." Ortiz would get word to Benito.

"Sure." The phone on the other end thudded against the bar. Salsa music blared in the background.

"Who is this?" a new voice said.

"Doesn't matter who it is." He checked his watch.

"What's this about the king's sister?" Ortiz's English was heavily accented.

Dane looked at the pictures of Nancy and him. His anger had gotten him this far and it would see him through until the end. "I'm making a booze run from Miami to New York when I stop in this small town in Virginia off I-81. While I'm drinking my coffee at a diner, I see a chick that looks like the king's sister."

Silence echoed on the other end of the line for a good ten seconds. In the background he heard the blend of percussion and drums playing.

Benito had promised five million to anyone who could find Elena.

"Don't even joke, bro," Ortiz said. "The king is a little crazed when it comes to his baby sister."

"I'm not joking. She looks different. Her hair is short, dyed blond like Gwen Stefani, but the face is a dead ringer."

"Why don't you just tell the king yourself?" Ortiz said.

"Oh no, man. I stay away from him. I don't want any part of his stuff. You pass on the good news."

"You're passing up a hell of a lot of money."

"Just tell him Brinkman might need a favor one day." Brinkman was an alias he'd used when he'd been undercover in Miami a couple of years ago.

"You sure it is her?"

"Yeah. She's a hard woman to forget."

"Thanks for the tip." The line went dead.

Dane could almost picture the cockroach now, scrambling out of his hovel in the Miami club. He'd be on his way now to find the next rat in the chain to Benito, ready to trade his information for money or a favor down the road.

It would take a day or two for Ortiz's information

to work up through the chain of Benito's command—
the mobster trusted few, and every bit of information
was screened before presented to Benito. But by the
middle of the week, Benito would receive the news.
And he would send his people to check out the story.
And with luck, would follow shortly after that.

Kristen was in grave danger now.

Lucian was watching her house for the moment.
But as savvy as the computer guy was, he was accustomed to working from the shadows. He'd never dealt
with the likes of Benito and his men face-to-face.

No, Dane had put Kristen in direct danger and he
would see to it she stayed safe.

He checked his watch. The sooner he got back to
her the better.

Chapter 9

Kristen was waiting in the front entryway for Cambia when she caught her reflection in the Plexiglas Yoga Studio sign that hung behind the reception desk. She ran her hand through her short hair. It still startled her and she wondered if she'd ever get to the point where she recognize herself in the mirror again

She frowned at the black roots. They were getting too long. She'd have to find a drugstore tomorrow and buy more hair dye.

She'd been so careful, and she didn't want something as foolish as hair color to trip her up.

Her outfit was beyond simple: jeans, a white

T-shirt and black sandals she'd bought at the Goodwill in North Carolina.

By all standards, she'd come down in the world. She had next to nothing and each day was an unknown. But in truth, she had never felt better. Benito was out of her life and the taste of freedom was so much sweeter than any expensive champagne Benito had paid for.

This was her life. All that she had, she'd earned. No one was paying doormen to get her to the front of the line. No one was feeding her compliments so they could get to her brother. This new life of hers wasn't perfect by any stretch of the imagination, but it was all hers and she was proud of it.

The rumble of Dane's truck pulled her out of her thoughts. She checked her watch. Seven on the dot. Her stomach fluttered as she watched him climb out of the cab. He'd changed into a white collared shirt, worn khakis and his work boots. His hair was wet from a shower and he'd shaved. He moved round to the front of the truck, his swagger hinting at military service.

For the first time in months she wished she'd had a bit of perfume to dab between her ears and maybe a tube of lipstick to brighten her lips. So much had changed in her life, but the streak of vanity had not vanished.

She went outside. "Right on time," she said. She smiled as she closed and locked the front door.

Even white teeth flashed. "I'm a stickler for time."

She moved down the steps, savoring the way he looked at her. Many men had leered at her in her life and she'd ignored most. Since Carlos, only Dane's intense gaze made her knees feel weak.

All day, she'd thought about when she'd kissed Dane. She'd chocked up the insanity of those kisses to loneliness and the need to feel connected to someone else. But now she knew she'd have been drawn to Dane even if she still had the legion of acquaintances and money she'd once had.

Dane Cambia stood out in a crowd.

"So where are we going?" he said, meeting her on the sidewalk. "You said there is a deli close by?"

"It's called Winston's. Sheridan told me about it. It's very good."

He squeezed her hand gently. "Then let's go."

When they reached the car, she hesitated and waited for him to open the door. He started around the front of the car until he saw her standing there. "Everything okay?"

Kristen realized her blunder. *Elena* would have expected a man to open her door but *Kristen* never would have. For nine months, she'd denied all things feminine. But since Dane had walked into her life, she'd been very aware that she was a woman.

Feeling a little foolish, she pretended to fix her

shoe and then reached for the door handle. "My shoelace needed tying."

"Right." A smile lifted the edge of his lips. He didn't believe her.

Kristen sat in the front seat, examining the interior, hoping for insight into the man. It was neat, organized. A large empty convenience-store coffee cup sat in the cup holder and there was an uneaten pack of Nabs tucked in the side pocket of his seat.

Without saying a word, he started the car and put it into Drive. Soon he was moving down the street. "Which way?"

"Take your first left." She'd only been in town two weeks but she'd already learned the streets, a habit she'd developed since she'd been on the run. Always good to know the escape routes.

She directed him through two more turns and within minutes he'd pulled into the deli lot. This time she opened her door without hesitating and met him on his side of the car. Together they walked toward the front entrance, where he reached the door first and opened it for her. As she entered he pressed his hand into the small of her back. The protective gesture pleased her more than it should have.

The deli was filled with round blue tables surrounded by scuffed chairs. A large glass case filled with meats, cheeses, pickles and breads dominated the front of the room. Above the counter a chalk-drawn menu hung on the wall. In the corner an old-style jukebox played John Cougar Mellencamp's "Jack and Diane."

Kristen and Cambia each placed their orders and when they reached the register, she dug her money out of her pocket.

"This is on me," Cambia said.

"No," she said firmly. "I pay my own way." It was another habit she'd developed since she'd been on the run. She didn't want to be dependent on anyone, nor did she want to owe anyone anything.

He pulled out his worn leather wallet. "Kristen, I insist."

She straightened out her ten-dollar bill. "As do I."

She met the cashier's gaze and pointed to the Reuben and water. "These are mine."

"No, I'm paying for it all," Dane said to the cashier.

The teenaged clerk glanced between the two of them as if he wasn't sure who to obey. Kristen remained firm, but it wasn't until Cambia gave the clerk the nod to take Kristen's money that he did.

Cambia paid for his meal. He followed her to a small table by the large glass front window that looked out onto the square of old town.

Kristen took her time wiping the table clean with a napkin, removing her food from her tray and arranging her napkin. Dane grinned as he watched her. "You take your meals seriously."

She blushed under his gaze. In the old days sit-down, formal meals were common, and she took them for granted; but now she treated a real meal as an event. Simple pleasures. "Yes, I know. I am a bit foolish when it comes to my meals. But I believe we eat with our eyes first and that it's important to have a proper table setting."

He sat down and stared at her, his meal untouched.

"You don't belong in a place like this."

Kristen shook her head. "Yes. I do."

"You're not a kid off the streets. You were born to money."

She unfolded her paper napkin and smoothed it over her lap. "I don't know what you mean."

He leaned forward, lowering his voice a fraction. "Come on. You walk like you are the queen of England, you never have a hair out of place even when you're working and you just spent five minutes setting the table in a simple deli. Let's face it, you don't belong in a place like this."

She glanced around the room. The deli was filled with mostly young college kids in worn T-shirts, jeans and flip-flops. The guy behind them, a tall lanky kid with mustard stains on a tie-dyed shirt was already halfway through his sandwich and his chips were gone.

"You're wrong." She didn't want to talk about herself. She sipped her cup of water and shifted tactics. "I've been wondering why you showed up so early today?"

Expressionless, Dane bit into a chip. "Yeah?"

She set her cup down. "And I think I know why."

He picked up his turkey club. "That so?"

Feeling awkward, she hesitated. "Are you living in your car?"

His eyes widened. "What?"

"It's nothing to be ashamed of," she rushed to say.

Amusement flickered in his eyes. "Why would you think that?"

"Because you just showed up this morning. It was almost as if you had been parked outside overnight."

He stared at her, saying nothing. Men could be proud, vain creatures and she suspected she'd offended him. "I'm not judging. I'm half on the streets myself. Fact is, I have been on the streets several times these last few months."

"Why have you been on the streets?" he said.

She shook her head. "No, you've done that a couple of times."

"What?"

"Turned the conversation back to me when you don't want to talk about yourself."

"Who just turned the conversation around a second ago?"

"That is beside the point. Why don't you talk about yourself?"

"Maybe you are getting too personal."

That caught her short. Embarrassment turned her cheeks red. "Perhaps I have grown too forward during these last few months. I didn't used to be like that."

He shrugged. "You are direct, I'll give you that."

She picked a piece of bread off her sandwich and popped it in her mouth. "Look, you don't have to tell me where you are living, but I can tell you where there is acceptable and cheap housing near here."

Her offer seemed to bother him. "Why would you help me? You don't even know me."

"I like you," she said honestly. "If you need money or a place to stay, I have a little saved up."

The fact that she had money seemed to worry him. "Don't tell people you have money."

"I'm not telling *people*. I'm telling *you*. I decided sometime today when I was dragging lumber to the Dumpster that you are a good man."

Disapproval darkened Dane's eyes. "Don't bet on it."

* * *

Dane hadn't counted on the fact that Kristen had money. Money equaled mobility. And he didn't want her mobile now.

But that was not a problem he could solve now, so he tucked it away, refusing to worry. He kept the rest of the evening light. They talked about music, the construction business and even politics, but neither offered any more personal information. Light and impersonal suited them both.

Dane drove Kristen back to the Yoga Studio and walked her up to the front door. Under the glow of the porch light, he waited as she dug the key out of her purse and opened the front door.

The take-out bag dangling from her arm, she faced him and smiled. "I had a good time."

He was sorry the evening was going to end. "Me too."

Without thinking, he raised his hand to her cheek and touched her blond hair. He traced her jawline and then her lips. He wanted to taste her again.

Kristen stared up at him, her full, moist lips slightly parted. "I made the first move last time. Now it's your turn."

Dane traced her brow with his fingertip. "I want to."

"Then do it," she said softly.

Dane tensed and released his jaw. He leaned

forward and pressed his lips to hers. Soft. Supple. Those lips drew him in and before he realized it, he wrapped his arm around her and deepened the kiss. The take-out bag poked his ribs so he pulled it out of her hand and set it on the porch.

Her scent wrapped around him. A soft moan rumbled deep in her chest as she pressed her breasts against his chest. She wanted him.

His tongue moved inside her mouth, caressing the velvet folds. Her hands pressed against his chest and she grabbed handfuls of his shirt and pulled him closer as if she wanted them to melt into each other.

Dane wanted to take her upstairs and make love to her right now. The primitive urge burned in his veins, making it difficult for him to think of anything else. His erection pressed against her as he kissed her harder.

But when he thought the need would sweep all reason from his mind, he found the strength to pull back. As much as he wanted her, he needed to stay objective. "I better get going."

Confusion darkened her eyes as she moistened her lips. "I don't want you to leave."

"It's not good to mix business and pleasure."

His rejection surprised her, and the hurt showed in her eyes.

He squeezed her shoulder and then stepped back. "When the job is done, Kristen. When the job is done."

Chapter 10

There was a storm brewing. And Kristen couldn't sleep. She'd lain awake for nearly an hour, listening to the creaks and moans of the old building as the wind washed over the house.

Soon the rains would come and make the air smell clean again.

Oddly, she felt fresh tonight and didn't need the rains to bathe away her past and worries. Memories of Antonio didn't consume her. Instead, she thought only of Dane. He'd brought *life* into her life.

She'd enjoyed their dinner together. It had been fun just to talk to someone over a good meal. Their laughter had rejuvenated her soul.

Why she'd thought to ask him about his living arrangements was beyond her. His life was none of her business. But she cared about him. He was a lost soul like her, belonging to no one. A kindred spirit.

He'd told her not to trust him.

But she did.

It made no sense. Trusting a near stranger defied all logic and reason. But the connection she felt between them was very real.

When he'd broken the kiss tonight, she'd felt lost.

"You are being a silly, lonely woman," Kristen told herself. "Your hormones are driving you now, not your mind."

Irritated, she sat up. If sleep would not come, then she would work. There were still piles of drywall dust and splinters in the soon-to-be meditation/tearoom. Perhaps a little sweeping would center her mind.

Kristen slept fully dressed, a habit she'd adopted since she'd fled the safe house. She turned on the hall lights and moved down the steps, flipping on more lights as she entered each new section of the house.

She went into the room under construction and grabbed the broom. As she swept the dust into neat piles, she tried not to think about Dane or whether he would be in her life a week from now.

Outside, a crack of thunder and a flash of lightning made her jump. The storm was going to be a big one.

She swept the debris into the dustpan and dumped it into an empty paper grocery bag. Within an hour the entire room and entry hallway was clean.

Lifting the grocery bag, Kristen headed back through the studio to the door that led to the alley. She unlatched the back door, glanced left and then right and hurried to the Dumpster. Lightning cracked. Fat rain droplets started to fall.

As she dashed back, she heard a can hit the ground.

She whirled around, her fists raised, her heart hammering in her chest. Her eyes strained in the darkness to see who was out there.

Another clap of thunder roared across the sky. Seconds later, lightning flashed again. In that moment of near daylight brightness, she saw Crystal sitting in the alley, her back pressed against the brick wall.

The girl had her feet tucked under her and she clutched her backpack. She held her coat up against her for warmth.

Kristen looked again down the alley, fearing Tony was close. There was no sign of him. "Crystal."

The girl brushed stringy blond hair from her face. "Go way. I'm trying to sleep."

Fat droplets hit Kristen. Soon, they'd both be soaked. And yet she walked toward the girl, her heart softening even as her mind screamed that the girl was trouble. Lord, but she didn't need more problems on her plate.

And still, she heard herself say, "It's raining. Why don't you come inside? I'll make you tea."

Crystal didn't move. "No, thanks, I like this spot."

More rain started to fall. Kristen hugged her arms over her chest. "I have half a sandwich left over from dinner. It's good." She'd intended to eat the food for her own lunch and dinner tomorrow, but the girl needed it more now.

Crystal sniffed. "What kind of sandwich?"

"A Reuben. Corned beef."

Crystal moistened her lips. "Okay. But I'm not staying long."

"Stay as long as you like."

Kristen watched the girl rise, clutching her backpack as she moved. She let the girl pass before following her into the building. Immediately, the quiet energy of the house/studio changed. Turmoil swirled around the girl.

Crystal nervously patted her thigh. "So where's the sandwich?"

Kristen checked the lock on the back door. "Up the back stairs in my apartment."

Crystal peered up the lighted stairway. "You live here?"

"For the last couple of weeks."

"I wondered why Sheridan was spending so much more time at the youth center."

"I open for her now so she doesn't have to get up so early."

Adjusting her backpack on her shoulder, Crystal started up the stairs. When she reached the top landing she waited for Kristen to open the door to her apartment and then peered inside as if she half expected someone to pounce on her. "It's small."

"It's all I need."

"When I graduate from college and I get my own place it's going to be *big*. Vaulted ceilings, huge windows and carpet so thick your feet sinks into it."

"Sounds nice."

Crystal set her backpack on the small round table. "It is. And it's going to be at the beach. I saw a house on HGTV just a couple of weeks ago that was exactly what I wanted."

Kristen moved to the refrigerator and opened it. She pulled out the white foam take-out box. The house she'd shared with her brother had been enormous and had overlooked the ocean. The view had been stunning; she'd been miserable. "Where do you live now?"

"On the streets sometimes but now mostly at the shelter."

Kristen cut the sandwich in half, sprinkled chips around it and set it in front of Crystal. "Why are you on the streets tonight?"

"I got to the shelter too late tonight. They lock the doors at ten and don't open them again until 6:00 a.m. If Sheridan had been there she'd have let me in, but when that dweeb Charlie is in charge there is no way I get in. He doesn't bend the rules at all."

"Why were you late?"

"Went by to see my mom. Big mistake. We got into a fight."

"Sorry." Home should have been the safe place to fall but it wasn't for Crystal. Just as it had never been for Kristen since her parents died. "You can stay here tonight if you want. The sofa pulls out into a bed."

The girl bit into the sandwich and quickly took a second bite. Kristen noticed she was wafer-thin and wondered when she'd eaten last.

"I don't know if I should stay," Crystal said.

Kristen took a seat at one of the two chairs at the table. "Suit yourself."

Crystal set down her book bag but didn't sit. A tattered copy of *Hamlet* stuck out of the back pocket. "You got anything to drink?"

"Water. Hot tea."

"Hot tea."

As Kristen rose to make the tea, she nodded to the book. "You read Shakespeare?"

"It's a school assignment. I've already read it twice."

That surprised Kristen. "How do you like it?"

"Kinda lame, but I've got to figure out what drives that stupid prince if I hope to ace the class."

Another surprise. "You make good grades?"

"A's and a couple of B's." Pride mingled with the anger and defiance.

"That's great."

Crystal cocked an eyebrow. "Don't look so shocked."

"I'm not."

Crystal snorted. "Most people just assume I'm a screwup. They don't look past the fact my folks are drunks. And Tony, well, hanging out with him didn't do me any favors. But I got dreams."

Kristen put a tea bag in a cup, filled it with water and put it in the microwave. She set it for two minutes. "Sit."

Crystal glanced at her, defiance in her eyes. But to Kristen's surprise the girl didn't argue. She sat, a quarter sandwich in one hand and a chip in the other.

"So, you gonna tell me I've set my sights too high?" Crystal asked.

How many times had her brother told her that? "I admire you."

The comment surprised Crystal. "Why?"

"You haven't given up on your dreams. One day I want to go to college, too."

"You haven't been? You look like college, money."

"The money is long gone and college wasn't in the cards for me."

"Why not?"

"My brother didn't want me to go, so I didn't."

The microwave dinged. Kristen pulled out the hot cup, gingerly set the tea bag aside for another cup later and handed her the mug.

Crystal finished the sandwich. She cupped her cold hands around the mug. "Thanks."

Kristen sat down across from her. Under the fading makeup she could see the sprinkle of freckles over the bridge of her nose. Her youthful skin was as smooth as porcelain. She wondered what the girl would look like in five years.

The teen sipped the tea. "You're staring at me."

Kristen averted her gaze. "Sorry." She decided not to push advice on the kid now. "So do you want to stay here tonight?"

Crystal shrugged. "Whatever."

The energy Kristen had felt earlier had faded. Her muscles ached from the hard work as exhaustion set into he bones. "Is that a yes or a no?"

The girl shrugged. "Yeah, sure, whatever."

Teenagers were supposed to be difficult. They pushed you beyond your limits. She'd certainly done that to her mother.

Kristen rose. "I'll make the pull-out bed."

"Why are you doing this?" Crystal stared down at her faded purple backpack, picking at a flower-shaped patch. "You have no reason to be nice to me."

"I don't know. Maybe because I've spent too much time just thinking about myself and what's best for me. Maybe I'm tired of that. Maybe I think you could use a friend to lean on."

"So I'm your fixer-up project?"

Kristen laughed. "I wouldn't go that far. I'm hardly in a position to fix anyone. I'm barely taking care of myself. But I can give you a safe place to sleep tonight and something to eat."

Crystal was silent for a moment. "No one, except Sheridan, has ever gone out of their way for me."

"That's too bad. Because you seem like a decent kid who's made a couple of crappy choices."

"You sound like a social worker."

"Sorry. I'll try and watch that."

"Thanks."

Kristen began to make up the bed for Crystal. "By the way, Hamlet had conflicting motivations. Integrity versus revenge."

Crystal nodded, smiled. "Thanks."

They got into their beds and Kristen turned off the light. Soon, through the darkness she heard Crystal's deep, even breathing. A vague feeling of well-being washed over her before she fell asleep.

Kristen woke up before dawn and immediately sensed something was wrong. She sat up and looked around the room.

The first thing she noticed was Crystal's unmade bed. She sat up and wiped the sleep from her eyes. She half expected to see the girl stumble out of the bathroom. But after a few minutes passed and there was no sign of the girl, she got up and checked around the apartment.

She quickly realized that Crystal was gone. And a second later discovered the cash she'd kept tucked in her backpack was missing.

It was every cent she had in the world.

Chapter 11

Friday, May 18, 7:02 a.m.

Again Kristen tore through the contents of her neatly packed knapsack, looking for the small change purse where she kept all her money. She checked the outside pockets. Nothing.

She straightened and jabbed her fingers through her hair. "Damn it," she muttered.

Crystal must have taken the money sometime last night. Normally, Kristen didn't sleep so hard but last night, after the day of exhausting work and several hours of insomnia, she'd fallen into a deep sleep, void of the usual nightmares.

Frustrated, she dumped the contents of her knapsack out on her unmade bed. She rifled through her belongings a second time. Her purse was missing.

The kid had played her. Big-time.

Trust was an overrated commodity. And she'd be wise to remember that.

Kristen grabbed her keys to the studio. She needed to find Crystal. Her first thought was the youth shelter. It would be open again now and Crystal stayed there quite a bit.

The early morning air was cold, and a dewy chill snaked down her spine as she walked down the street toward the youth shelter, located in an old row house three blocks away.

Kristen hurried up the brick steps and knocked on the door. Loud music thundered inside. Sheridan had said the shelter allowed music but she'd not realized it could be so loud and so early in the day. She knocked again.

Folding her arms over her chest, she glanced over her shoulder. The street was quiet. Seconds later she heard footsteps moving toward the door inside the shelter and the deadbolt unlock.

Standing in the doorway was a man not much older than her. Heavyset, he sported a thick beard and wire-rim glasses that covered soft blue eyes. He checked his watch. "Can I help you?"

"I'm looking for Crystal." She didn't know the girl's last name and hoped the man would not ask her for it.

"Are you family?"

"No. I'm a…friend. A good friend."

The man studied her with cautious eyes. "I can't release information about my kids to non family members."

She tried to keep her body relaxed, her voice free of worry. "Are you Charlie?"

He eyed her suspiciously. "Yeah."

"I'm a friend of Sheridan's."

Charlie lifted a brow. "You know how many times I've heard that one?"

Frustrated, she clenched her fists. "Look, I just want to ask Crystal a question."

The man shook his head. "Sorry. You ain't family then you don't get in. I got my hands full as it is and I don't want trouble."

"I don't want trouble. I just want to talk to Crystal. Just for a minute. *One minute.*" Desperation had crept into her voice this time.

He started to close the door, but she blocked it with her foot.

"She stole money from me. It was all I had. It took me eight months to save that money."

His eyes reflected his doubt. "If I had a dime for the sob stories I've heard, I'd be a rich man."

Clenched fists at her side, she shouted, "I'm not lying."

He shook his head. "I can't help you. Now get your foot out of my door."

Kristen hated feeling helpless and out of control. "All I want to do is *talk* to her."

"Sorry." He nudged her out of the way and closed the door.

Kristen stood on the porch for almost a minute, hoping Charlie would see her, take pity and open the door. He did neither.

The morning cold swept through her body and she was bone weary. She hugged her arms around her chest. These last few months she'd been inching her way toward a real life but now it was gone. She had nothing.

Kristen swallowed back tears and lifted her chin.

She would not give up. She'd survived so much up until now. Losing the money hurt, but she would find a way to rebuild.

As she started down the steps, she had an odd sensation that someone was staring at her.

Across the street a young couple held hands and kissed. Several doors down a man walked an old dog. But none of those people were looking at her. And still, the feeling wouldn't go away.

"Who's out there?" she said.

Nothing.

Kristen glanced back at the door. Charlie wasn't going to let her in no matter what. She decided to make a run for the studio. It was only a few blocks and if she hurried she'd be there in minutes.

Kristen glanced up and down the street one last time. Nothing out of the ordinary.

And yet nothing felt right.

When Kristen arrived at the studio ten minutes later, she found a young woman knocking on the studio door. The woman was trying to peek past the curtains.

Kristen slowed her pace and tried to collect herself. "Can I help you?"

The woman turned. Red curls framed a heart-shaped face and alert blue eyes. She was wearing her yoga gear and holding her mat.

"Why haven't you opened up the studio yet? Class is going to be starting in ten minutes."

Kristen walked up the steps and moved past her to open the front door. "The studio is closed until next Monday." She pointed to the sign on the door.

The woman glanced from Kristen to the sign. Her annoyance deepened. "Crap. I forgot all about that. Sheridan told me but I zoned. I've had a killer deadline to make."

"Deadline?"

"Sorry. I'm Simone Brady. I'm Sheridan's friend."

The reporter. "I'm sorry. We're under construction. By next week the tearoom will be open." She hoped the nugget of information would make her feel better and coax her to leave.

It didn't. "The muscles between my shoulder blades are so tight you could bounce a quarter off them. And my head is pounding from all the tension. This is so not good."

Kristen couldn't muster sympathy. She'd just lost her life savings to a street kid. "I'm sorry. Sheridan isn't even in town."

Giving in to defeat, Simone sighed. "Hey, it's not your fault. And I'm sorry I snapped your head off. Deadlines turn me into Satan."

"It's okay."

Simone pushed manicured fingers through her shoulder-length red curls. "Hey, while I've got you, when will Sheridan be back?"

"Two days, if all goes well with her sister."

"Good. Did she tell you about the story I'm doing on the studio?"

"Yes."

"I'll be sending a photographer here to take photos at the first of the week."

"Will do." Not good.

Simone started to turn and leave then stopped as if remembering something. "You're going to be in the picture, too, aren't you?"

Kristen knew she'd not be available when the photographer showed up. And if Sheridan pressed she'd leave town. Even if she had to hitch a ride. "I don't think so."

"But you are the official studio staff."

"This is Sheridan's studio. I'm just temporary help."

"Sheridan said you are heaven sent. That you are already practically running the place."

Kristen opened the door and stepped inside. "She was being kind."

"The two of you standing in front of the sign will be a real eye-catcher."

Fear made her direct. "I don't want to be in the paper," she said.

"But think of the publicity for the studio. It will be great."

An uncomfortable tightness formed in the pit of Kristen's stomach. She could not have her picture in the paper. Period. "No."

Simone stared at her as if she were trying to read her thoughts. "Hey, I don't want to push anything on you. Just think about it."

"I don't mean to sound ungrateful. But I think it's best you focus solely on Sheridan."

Simone's eyes narrowed slightly. Kristen imagined her reporter's mind working overtime.

But at that moment, Dane Cambia's old truck rolled up in front of the studio. Its big, loud engine rumbled to a stop. He glanced up at them, frowned and got out of his truck. As he strode up the stairs, she noticed his gait was slightly stiff. He stopped just feet short of Simone.

The reporter watched the carpenter approach, a note of appreciation in her eyes. To Kristen's surprise, she felt a kick of jealousy.

Trying to pretend she wasn't a mass of nerves inside, Kristen smiled. "Simone, I'd like you to meet Dane Cambia. He is doing the renovation for the new tearoom. Dane, Simone Brady. She is a stringer for the *Post* and she's going to be doing a piece on the studio."

"Pleased to meet you, ma'am." The grin Dane tossed Simone irritated Kristen.

The reporter held out her hand and squeezed firmly when Dane took it. "I've been trying to talk Kristen into a photo for the paper. She and Sheridan are both stunners and a picture of them in front of the studio would sell a lot of papers."

Dane nodded. "Sounds like a good idea."

Simone smiled. "Convince Kristen. She's camera shy."

"You should let her take your photo." Dane winked at Kristen.

Kristen felt backed into a corner. "I'll think about it, okay?" Simone swung her yoga-mat case higher on her shoulder. "Well, I better get going. Since no yoga today, caffeine is in order." She grinned at Cambia. "You're new in town."

"Yep. Trying to build a book of business."

She arched an eyebrow, reached in her pocket and pulled out a card. "Call me. I know a couple of people who've bought older houses that are going to need work. You can toss in a bid."

He studied the card, fingering the edges. "Great."

"I'll help you set up some interviews."

Dane grinned as he tucked the card in his pocket. "Consider it done."

Simone said her goodbyes and walked down the steps to her red Mini. She got in the car, shoved the gear into first and drove off, grinding gears as she shifted to second.

Kristen felt relieved to see her go. The woman was too smart and too persistent. Dangerous.

Taking in a deep breath she turned her mind to the next problem at hand. Crystal. She wanted to run off looking for the girl but that would raise questions with Dane and the last thing she needed was more questions.

"You look like hell," Dane said.

Startled, she glanced up at him. "What? No, I'm fine."

"Your skin is as white as a ghost."

"I didn't sleep well," she lied.

"Have you eaten breakfast yet?"

"I'm not hungry." In truth her stomach was a mass of knots.

He jerked his thumb toward the truck. "I brought bagels and coffee."

His thoughtfulness touched her. "You didn't have to do that."

He waved off her concern as he headed to the truck to retrieve his goods. "I hate to eat alone. You're doing me a favor."

Kristen shook her head. She folded her arms over her chest. She'd eat simply because she didn't want to draw any more attention to herself. She needed time to think. To plan her next move.

Kristen was rattled, Dane observed. Her lips had flattened into a grim line and her attention was distracted. It wasn't just the fact that Simone had wanted to take her picture. That certainly would have been enough to shake her up. But it was more.

He'd seen her tear out early this morning to the youth shelter. What had happened?

He hadn't seen any sign of Benito's men and immediately suspected Crystal, whom he'd had Lucian investigate. The kid had lived at the shelter for several months, but she was smart, made straight A's in spite of a lousy home life.

If he had to bet he'd say Kristen had trusted the kid. It didn't take a psychic to see that Crystal had ripped her off.

"Do you like plain, potato or cinnamon-raisin?" he said, smiling.

She stepped aside so that he could move into the studio. "Any is fine."

"The coffee is Columbian. The strongest they have. I needed a jolt of the java today." Keeping his tone light didn't come naturally to him, but he'd stand on his head and sing Dixie if it meant keeping her close.

"Sounds good."

He moved into the soon-to-be tearoom. To his surprise the place was swept clean, pristine almost. "I told you not to worry with the broom. We're only going to mess it up today."

She closed the front door and entered the tearoom. "I couldn't sleep."

If she was broke, she was vulnerable. No cash. No quick ability to get out of town. "You look as nervous as a cat."

She managed a smile. "I'm not."

"Something happen last night?"

"No."

"Has Crystal been by again?"

Surprise darkened her eyes. "What makes you say that?"

"The kid ran to the studio the last time she was in trouble."

"No, she didn't come by."

Kristen was a bad liar. So it *was* Crystal.

She nodded to the floor. "We can sit picnic-style on the floor."

"Sure." Kristen always changed the subject when she was nervous. He decided he'd make things easy for her today. It was the least he could do.

She sat down on the floor in a cross-legged position. She moved with the grace and ease of a dancer.

Wincing, he lowered himself to the floor. His right hip ached and he didn't have the flexibility to cross his legs as she had. He settled for sitting with his back straight and leaning against a wall.

He handed her a cup of coffee. "You make that look so easy."

"Sitting?"

"Yeah." He shifted his weight off his left hip. Most days it didn't bother him, but too much time in the van had left him hurting.

She sipped her coffee. "Did you injure your hip?"

"A couple of years back."

"What happened?"

He could tell her that he'd been overseas on a recon mission, that there'd been an explosion and he'd taken shrapnel. But that was more information than he wanted to disclose. The less said the better. "Fell off a ladder while I was painting a house. Busted myself up pretty good. Could you show me a few stretches to ease the pain? I hear yoga is good for that kind of stuff."

She looked surprised by the request. "Sheridan says a lot of pain in our backs and legs comes from tight hips."

That was a new one for him. But if talking yoga erased the troubled look from her eyes, he'd do it. "Tight hips? Think you could help me out?"

"Sitting cross-legged will help open up the joints."

"There's got to be something else."

She sighed. "There are a few stretches she showed me."

He winked at her. "I guess you could show 'em to me, but then you've only been at this yoga thing a couple of weeks."

Challenge flashed in her eyes. "I've learned a few things. Come into the studio and I will show you a couple of stretches."

He could just picture himself now trying to twist into a yoga pose. "You're the boss."

She moved into the studio and, avoiding the large florescent overhead lights, turned on the soft wall sconces. Kristen stopped him before he could enter the room. "Take your shoes off."

"Why?"

"No shoes in the studio."

He glanced down at his scuffed work boots. "Right." Bending down, he undid the double knots in his laces and slipped off his boots. He set them outside the studio door and followed her inside.

Kristen went to the corner to the stack of unrolled mats and chose two along with a couple of blankets. She unrolled the mats and positioned them side by side.

"Come on over here and have a seat on the mat." To demonstrate she sat down with her feet sticking straight out. Her straight spine and legs made a perfect L. "This is called the staff pose."

Cambia felt like a fool but now was not the time to argue with her. So, he sat beside her and positioned himself like her.

To his surprise, the muscles in the backs of his legs and lower back were very tight. Stress was no doubt the culprit.

Kristen rose and came up behind him. She put her hand on the small of his back and with gentle pressure drew her hand up his spine, which forced him to sit an inch or two higher. "There you go."

Her soothing and calm voice coupled with her touch would have had him hardening if not for the discomfort in his back.

"Your shoulder blades are very stiff," she said.

He shoved out a breath. "Yep."

She chuckled. "That will ease when I show you how to stretch."

"You mean I'm not stretching yet?" Pride had him holding the position as she knelt behind him. He could run ten miles with a twenty-pound pack on his back, so he could damn well handle a few yoga poses.

As she adjusted his shoulders back, her breasts brushed against him. Why the hell had he agreed to this?

"This is a hard position to hold, especially if you have tight hamstrings. How far do you run?" she said.

"Five to ten miles a day when I can."

"Hopefully not on pavement." She took hold of his head and pulled up.

"Most of the time."

"The concrete will tear up your back. Stay to the dirt paths—as close to the earth as you can manage."

Her knowledge of physiology surprised him. "So when did you learn all this?"

"Sheridan. She's been teaching me a lot."

"You like it here, then?"

"Yes."

He might not have found her so quickly if she hadn't stayed here so long.

"Now, lean forward and touch your hands toward your knees," she said.

He did as she asked, swallowing a groan as his hamstrings pulled. "Damn."

"Does it hurt?"

"Yep."

"Then back off. It should never hurt."

Despite his discomfort, he held his position. "I'm not good at backing off."

She placed her callused hands over his as she tried to pull them back several inches. He tensed, not ready to let go. Her feminine scent wafted around him, making him almost forget he was hurting. Almost.

"You can't muscle into a stretch. Your body will only resist and make the work all the harder."

"Muscling is my specialty."

"Let go," she coaxed.

With an effort he did.

"Now try the stretch again," she said.

This time when he did, he found he could go deeper.

"See?" Kristen said.

He always gave credit where credit was due. "Okay, got it."

"There are hundreds of other stretches I could show you but I suspect you won't sit still for them."

He liked hearing her soft voice and having her close. He was half tempted to let her show him those hundreds of poses. But there was work to be done. "I can sit still for a couple more."

Surprised, she nodded. Sitting beside him, she demonstrated a pose she called the Pigeon pose. He felt goofy as hell, but to his amazement when he moved into the position the pounding in the back of his leg eased immediately. "You are a miracle worker. You must have been a healer in another life."

"The body doesn't need much if you are willing to listen. Or so Sheridan says."

Light came in through the window at the back of the room, casting a warm glow on her pale skin. He tried to remember how soft her skin felt when he'd touched her yesterday. She was only inches from him and he could easily reach over and touch her. He wondered if she'd kiss him again if he did.

Last night, he'd dreamed of her. Of taking her on this very floor, peeling off her gray pants and kissing her soft skin. She'd been willing and wanted, and had accepted, all of him as he'd pushed into her. She'd called out his name and dug her fingers into his back.

Sensing his thoughts, her gaze shifted, color rose in her cheeks. She rose and straightened. "We've got a full day's work ahead of us."

He cleared his throat. "Right."

Yesterday, she'd been ready to bed him; today the reserve was fully in place like a shield.

It was better that way.

Kristen had every right not to trust him.

Chapter 12

Kristen stood in front of the entryway mirror and glanced at her reflection, especially her dark roots. She shoved a shaky hand through her hair.

It was growing.

The emerging black strands were becoming more evident and hinted at a past she couldn't escape. In this moment, she looked so much like Elena.

Elena.

The hair would have to be cut soon and the roots

dyed. No traces of Elena could emerge. Elena had to stay buried in the past. However, with her money gone, she'd have to wait until Dane paid her tonight. Then she could slip off to the drugstore and buy the products she needed.

There was still no sign of Crystal. She'd searched again last night for the girl after the work-day ended, but nothing.

Kristen heard Dane's truck pull up. She moved to the front door and peeked through the blinds. Dane slid out of the driver's side seat and walked around to the back. He pulled out long planks of wood. The muscles in his arms bunched under his T-shirt. She touched her lips, remembering their kiss in the kitchen.

Lord help her, but she still wanted to touch him.

Shaking off the thought she unlatched the locks on the front door and opened it. "Good morning," she said.

He flashed a quick grin that made her a little giddy. "Good morning."

"Let me help you with that."

"I've got this one but there are others in the truck. How are your ribs?"

"Only a little sore today." She hurried down the stairs, pulled a board from the truck and headed back. She met him halfway on the sidewalk. "This wood is lovely. What is it for?"

"Benches. Sheridan called me last night. She

wants benches and shelves built into the wall. I'll install them before I paint."

Kristen hesitated. "You talked to Sheridan?"

"She said to let you know she'll be back in two days. She's also sorry she hasn't called you. Apparently, things have been a little crazy around her sister's house. The baby came late yesterday. I heard a toddler crying in the background. I think things are a little out of control."

It bothered Kristen that Sheridan hadn't called her. She thought of the woman as a friend. Silly, she thought. She'd known the woman two weeks. And like Dane said, she'd been busy.

Kristen got another board and started up the stairs. "I can imagine."

He grabbed two more pieces of lumber and caught up to her in the studio lobby. "So any more visits by Tony or Crystal?"

"No signs of Tony or Crystal." Just saying the girl's name reminded her of her own stupidity and soured her mood.

His gaze settled on her. "What's wrong?"

The comment surprised her. "What makes you think anything is wrong?"

"You get a distinct wrinkle right in the middle of your forehead when you are worried."

She raised her fingertips to her forehead and felt the

twin creases. She wanted to confide in him about Crystal and what had happened. She hadn't said anything yesterday but now she couldn't contain her thoughts. She needed a friend. "I lied to you yesterday."

"About what?"

She sighed. "Crystal. I let Crystal in the other night."

"Why?" His tone was neutral and not admonishing as she'd expected.

"I was dumping trash. She was in the alley. It was cold and raining, and she was huddled in a doorway. Anyway, I invited her in for the night."

"And?" His voice deepened with concern.

"She ate my food and she seemed to relax. The next day I woke up and she'd stolen by money." Frustration tightened her throat.

He frowned.

Sensing admonishment in his eyes, she rushed to say, "I shouldn't have fallen for her wounded-dove routine."

His dark gaze bore into her. "You were being kind."

"My brother always said I was a soft-hearted fool."

The mention of her brother seemed to catch him off guard. "It doesn't sound like your brother is such a nice guy."

"He's not."

"Do you want to tell me about him?"

She paused. She hadn't uttered anything about Antonio since she'd fled Florida. But now the urge to talk was strong. So many pent-up emotions begged to be spoken. "The less you know about my brother the better. He is a very dangerous man."

"I'm a big boy, Kristen. And I can take care of myself."

"Not where my brother is concerned. He is a very powerful, cruel man and I pray I never see him again."

"Is he the reason you're working for cash and living on the run?"

His dead-on insight startled her. "I'm not living on the run."

Dane stacked three boards on top of each other. "I know fear when I see it, Kristen, and you are loaded with it. You jump when a car door slams and you look as if you'd bolt at the first sign of trouble."

"I didn't realize I was so transparent," she muttered more to herself.

"You are to me and probably to Sheridan. Likely that's why she trusted you with so much."

She stared at the twisting grain of the wood. "This is not good."

"Hey, don't look so glum." He grinned. "Your secrets are safe with me."

"Are they?"

He cupped her face. "Yes."

When he touched her, her heart stopped for a moment. She couldn't breathe and every nerve in her body danced with excitement as it had the first time he'd touched her. Worries and doubts that should have surfaced and warned her away from this man stayed silent. All she felt was a bone-searing desire.

She reached up and laid her hands over his. The rough edge of his beard teased the smooth skin on the back of her hand. She traced a small scar that ran along his chin.

Dane captured her hand and drew it to his lips. He kissed her palm. She hissed in a breath.

Slowly, he lowered her hand and interlocked his fingers with hers. He leaned forward and kissed her on the mouth. Gently he teased her lips open with his tongue. Willingly she accepted him, leaning into the kiss and releasing into it all the passion that had welled inside her these long lonely months.

"This isn't a good idea," he said. His breath was hot against her cheek.

She felt so alive.

"It's the best idea I've had in months." She rose up on tiptoes and wrapped her arm around his neck, surrendering fully to the kiss. A moan rumbled in his chest as he banded his arm around her waist and pulled her against him. His erection pressed against her, sending an erotic thrill through her body.

He dropped his hand to her waist, slid it up her blouse. She drew in a quick breath as his knuckles brushed the underside of her sheer bra. He pinched her nipples, coaxing them into hard peaks. Warmth spread through her body.

She reached for his belt buckle and with trembling fingers fumbled with the worn metal until it came loose. She unsnapped the top of his jeans and slid her hand inside.

He growled with pleasure and pulled her hand free as if he could barely hold on to his composure. "So help me, I do want you."

"Good."

He closed and locked the front door and then in one easy move, he scooped her up and carried her to the tiny bed in her room.

Dane laid her in the center. The mattress sagged under his weight as he straddled her. He kissed her on the mouth before he pushed up her blouse and pressed his lips to her flat belly. He tugged at the drawstring of her yoga pants and then slid them off her narrow hips and past her knees. Without regard to where they landed, he tossed them on the floor.

Cool air brushed her naked skin and for a moment she felt exposed and self-conscious. But Dane gave her no time to dwell on her modesty. He kissed her belly again and then moved to her moist center. She arched her back, digging her fingers into his hair.

His bearded chin rubbed her naked flesh, sending bolts of desire through her body.

Dane lifted his head and she moaned her displeasure as he slid off the side of the bed and took off his pants. He produced a condom from his wallet. With quick, sure hands, he tore the package open and slid it on.

Kristen rolled on her side and savored the sight of him. Staring so boldly at him, she felt wanton.

When their gazes locked, his eyes darkened with so much desire, she could feel a blush warming her skin. In the next instant, he was on top of her, his heat pressing against her. She opened her legs, and needing no other invitation, he pressed inside her. She tensed.

It had been a very long time since she'd been with a man and her body was tight. A part of her felt disloyal to Carlos but a larger part was so hungry to experience life.

Sensing her reservation, Dane kissed her on the lips, giving her body time to grow accustomed to him before he started to move slowly inside of her, as if savoring every inch of her.

Quickly, her body became accustomed to him.

Desire banished all worries and doubts and swept her toward something great she'd never experienced but knew she wanted.

She lifted her hips, so that he entered her to the hilt. He kissed her on her mouth. The tension in his body told her how much he wanted her. She reveled in the powers of her femininity.

Kissing him back, she arched her breasts into his chest. He began to move faster. Within minutes, both were covered in sweat and hungry with passion.

She wanted to take this coupling slowly and savor each moment, but the need was too great. Unable to hold back, she held on to the desire until she thought she could take no more.

And then in one swift stroke the passion exploded in them. She arched her back, digging her fingers into his back and whispering his name as if it were a pledge.

Dane groaned his pleasure as she climaxed and gave in to his own needs. He collapsed against her. His heart hammered against her chest as he breathed against her ear.

She'd never felt more at peace. Never more whole. Kristen fell asleep in his arms, certain that her life was finally on track.

It felt good to trust again.

Chapter 13

Three tarot cards lay before Antonio Benito on the small terrace table covered with a white linen tablecloth. Bright, hot Miami sun shone down on him as a lithe, dark woman, Serena, sat across from him. She came to his house each day to read his tarot cards.

Ice clinked softly in Benito's Baccarat tumbler filled with bottled water. "So what do the cards say? Does it say anything about my sister?"

Serena, aware of Benito's reputation, spoke cautiously, as she always did. She despised the man but he fed her children and kept them safe so she remained loyal to him.

Serena tapped the center card. "This is the Ace of Cups. It reflects how you felt about yourself."

Benito sat a little straighter.

"It means Abundance, self-love and love for the world."

"Me love the world?" He laughed. "Perhaps, like a god loves the world he controls."

"You have great insight," she added, careful to keep her voice even. She had no wish to anger him. "The world is yours for the taking."

He grunted, satisfied. "What do the other cards say?"

"To the right of the Ace of Cups is the Chariot. In the Challenges position this means you will be tempted by a new and dangerous element."

"Like in business?"

Her long dark curls brushed her thin shoulders as she shook her head. "No, I sense this card refers to a personal matter."

Benito leaned forward. "Does this have to do with my sister?"

Here she walked a fine line. She knew Benito wanted desperately to find his sister. Yet to give him hope and have it dashed was too risky. But today, she'd heard some of his men talking. The buzz of excitement hummed in their voices and she'd heard Elena's name mentioned. "I believe that it does." She tapped the last card. "The Six of Wands in the Situation position. You have the power to stir up long-term change."

"Is that all you have?" He was annoyed.

She kept her face devoid of emotion and tapped her ringed index finger on the last card. She needed to give him more. "This change could have to do with your sister."

"Such as?"

"If you are to have an answer it will come soon. Very soon."

He leaned forward. "When!"

"That is all the cards gave me today. I wish there was more."

Frustration seemed to eat at him. "The cards can be so fickle. Kind one day, cruel the next."

"It is the way, no matter how much we will it otherwise. The cards reveal themselves as they choose."

A heavy silence settled between them. "I need my sister back. She is all the family that I have. We are meant to be a united front."

"The day will come," she said.

He swiped the cards off the table, sending them fluttering to the tiled floor. "Leave."

Serena dropped to her knees and quickly gathered her cards. If only she could see into the future. She would tell him what she saw. But like everyone else in Benito's life, she danced on eggshells and prayed he didn't get angry with her.

Benito listened to the click of Serena's high heels as she hurried across the tiled floor. He'd begun to think that the woman was as lost as he and of no further use to him.

Sunlight winked on the monogrammed gold signet ring on his left pinky as his gaze shifted to the crystal blue Atlantic. Sailboats and yachts dotted the horizon. Sun sparkled on their white hulls.

Elena loved to sail. He'd bought her a fine thirty-foot yacht for her twentieth birthday. She'd loved it, spending hours sailing the open waters.

His Elena also loved the hot sun and the white sand. She would have so loved to be on the beach today.

A sudden crushing sadness overcame him. It had been over a year since he'd seen his beloved sister.

The lonely months had allowed his temper to cool. He no longer dreamed of strangling her until she was dead, as he had in those days after she'd gone to the police. Now he simply wanted her back.

She was his only family, his blood. And he would move heaven and earth to get her back. No matter what it cost. And yet what more could he do? The reward for her was five million. Every contact he had in the world was searching for her. And yet there was nothing, as if she'd fallen off the face of the earth.

The world could be a cruel place and his Elena was unwise in its ways. Last night he'd dreamed of her crying and alone, calling out to him for help.

He prayed nothing bad had befallen her.

After several minutes he was aware that his second in command—Manuel Ortiz—stood behind him. The short, stocky man never disturbed him unless it was important.

"What is it?" Benito said without turning around.

Manuel, his head bowed, stepped forward. In his hand he held a piece of white paper. "We've heard from a man. He is of no consequence normally, but this time he might have something of use."

Benito sipped his water, his eyes trained on the boats. He prayed Elena had enough to eat, that she had a warm place to sleep.

Manuel, a file tucked under his arm, tugged on the cuffs of his white linen shirt. "He has heard that Elena might be in Virginia."

Benito's heart hammered faster but he kept his face impassive. There had been sightings of Elena before but all had been false leads. Bitter disappointment had eaten at him each time. He'd learned not to show his excitement, yet he still could not stop his heart from racing like a wild stallion. "We have heard claims like this before."

"That's why I wanted to check it out first before I came to you."

"And?"

"I sent a man up north yesterday. He took pictures. When I saw the pictures, I thought you needed to see them." Manuel opened the white folder he'd been holding and laid the color photos on the glass tabletop.

Benito drew in a breath and steeled himself before he glanced down.

At first, disappointment washed over him. He saw only the woman's blond hair and her too-thin frame clad in simple clothes. She stood in front of a shabby youth shelter.

But a second look revealed more. He saw Elena's sharp brown eyes. He recognized the firm line of her proud jaw. Her long delicate hands.

Dios. He'd found his sister.

His pulse quickening, he shuffled through the photos. There were dozens just like the first.

He studied the woman in the photo again. He traced the blond hair, annoyed that she'd cut and colored the dark hair he'd taken such pride in. But hair would grow. Time would erase the changes she'd made to herself just as it had wiped away his anger toward his only sister. Time would fix everything. Soon life would be the way it was before Carlos had swept into her life.

She was his family. *His blood.* And her place was at his side.

Benito closed the file. "Get my plane ready. I am going to Virginia."

Kristen lay on her side, her breasts nestled next to Dane's side. Her hand lay draped over his broad chest and she could feel the steady beat of his heart under her palm.

This was the first time she'd really seen him relaxed, and she realized she liked looking at him. He had a strong jaw and the dark stubble on his chin combined with the longer bangs made him look a bit like a pirate.

She traced a heart on his chest.

He sighed but didn't open his eyes. "I thought you were asleep."

She smiled. "Moments like this are so rare. I don't want to waste them sleeping."

He laid his hand over hers and squeezed gently. "I wish it could be different."

"How?" Their lovemaking had been perfect. "I thought it was ideal."

He opened his eyes and looked at her. This close she could see the splashes of gray in his blue eyes. "You've not been with a man for a long time."

"Only one before you."

"I can't believe a beautiful woman like you didn't have a legion of admirers."

"My brother is overprotective. He chased most suitors away."

Absently he rubbed her bare leg. "You've mentioned your brother before."

"He's a complex man." Benito was the last person she wanted to talk about. "I'm better off with distance between the two of us."

"Has he hurt you?" There was anger in his voice now.

"Everything he did he thought was for my own good." She swallowed a lump in her throat. "But at times he was quite cruel."

Dane pulled her against his side. "I'll never let him hurt you."

The force behind the words surprised her. "I don't ever intend on seeing him again." She propped her chin on her hands pressed against his chest. "I don't want to talk about my brother or anyone else outside of this room."

He brushed the bangs off her forehead. "The world out there is waiting for us."

"I know. But for now, this moment, it does not exist. It's just us in our own world."

A smile tipped the edge of his mouth. "We have work to do today."

"Do we have to work today? It's been so long since I really enjoyed a day." When she was with Dane she didn't feel afraid. The past was a distant memory that didn't have the power to hurt her.

Dane traced his knuckle along her jawline. "Your offer is very tempting."

She grinned. "Good."

He hugged his arms around her. "I don't deserve you."

She stared into his eyes, trying to read his thoughts. "What makes you say that?"

He hesitated and seemed to choose his words carefully. "I don't have much to offer. You deserve so much more than I can give."

"I don't want anything. I just want to be happy and you make me happy."

He frowned.

There was so much to this man she didn't know. Like her, he had demons. But she knew under the sadness there was a good man. "What is your idea of the perfect day?"

He smiled, perplexed by the sudden change of conversation. "I don't know."

"Would you go to a fine restaurant, go to a football game or climb a mountain?"

His hand slid down under the sheet covering her back down to her bottom. He squeezed gently. She could feel his arousal pressing against her. "This day is damn near perfect."

Excitement simmered inside her. "But where would you go?"

He shook his head. Absently, he moved his hand up and down her leg. "I don't know. I haven't thought about fun in so long I wouldn't know what to do. How about you? What's your perfect day?"

She chuckled. "You would be there, of course."

He squeezed her bottom again in response.

"We would huddle on the couch and watch old movies if it were a rainy day. And if it were lovely, we'd go to the beach and I would lie in the hot sun and listen to the ocean waves. I haven't seen a movie or been to the beach in so long."

"One day I will take you to the beach and to the movies."

Childish excitement bubbled inside her. "Truly?"

"When this job is over, if you're still interested in going with me, I will take you."

Excitement bubbled inside her. "Of course I will still be interested in going with you. Why wouldn't I want to go with you?"

"Things change."

"Not that much."

He raised his head and kissed her on the lips. He tasted salty. His lips were soft. "I hope so."

She drew more shapes on his chest with her index finger. The future was too dark and frightening so she chose to concentrate on now. "That sounds so ominous."

"You don't know anything about me."

"Then tell me everything."

He stared at her. There was something behind his eyes—something dark, painful. "For now, the less said the better. In time, I'll tell you more about myself."

But she couldn't let it go. She'd spent the night with this man—made love to him twice—and sensed that she was starting to care about what happened to him. "What brought you to Lancaster Springs?"

"Work." Even the terse word sounded guarded.

"There's more to it than that." A black thought entered her mind. "I'm starting to wonder if there isn't a Mrs. Cambia and a couple of kids back home—wherever that is." The thought made her sick.

He rolled on his side and faced her. "No wife. No kids. Just you."

The information offered a measure of comfort but didn't banish all the worries. "No, there's more. I see it in your eyes. I see the anger. Something is chewing at you."

He sat up slowly and stabled fingers through his mussed hair. "You're imagining things."

There'd been a time when she might have believed

him and ignored her worries. She'd done it with Benito a thousand times, until the facts of who and what he was could no longer be ignored. "I've learned to trust my instincts. You are hiding something."

He released a deep breath. "I'm not sure what you want me to say. We all have our secrets. You haven't told me everything about yourself."

"True." She kept secrets to protect him. Benito had destroyed the only other man that she'd loved.

He ran his hand over her bare shoulder. "Are you ready to share yours with me?"

"Mine are quite ugly, Dane. You don't want to know them." She feared if he knew the truth of her past he'd reject her. Others had in the past.

Shadows slashed across his face as he stared down at her. "You can tell me anything."

Oh, the urge to let all the hurt and pain tumble out was so strong. Thoughts of Antonio's viciousness kept her quiet. "Maybe we both need time before we're ready to talk."

He cupped her face. "You've grown pale. Something has scared you."

"Ghosts from the past. They can't hurt me anymore, but they still frighten me sometimes."

He kissed her gently on the forehead. "I won't let ghosts or monsters hurt you, Kristen. No matter what happens, that I swear."

She felt so safe when he was close. "I know you'd never hurt me." She smiled. "I guess we'll both have to trust the other and wait until the time is right to talk about our pasts."

Instead of answering, he kissed and made love to her with such passion. It was almost as if he was afraid he was going to lose her.

Chapter 14

The instant Dane entered his darkened hotel room he knew he wasn't alone. He reached for the .32 he kept strapped to his ankle, pulled back the hammer and flicked on the light.

In the corner by the window sat Lucian Moss. The man's eyes were closed and his fingers folded over his chest. He looked perfectly at ease.

Dane lowered his gun. "You're lucky I didn't shoot you."

Lucian opened his eyes. He wasn't the least bit ruffled by the comment. "You're late."

"I took Kristen out to diner." Her scent was still on him and he couldn't stop thinking about touching her. Guilt ate at his gut. He should never have touched her.

"You mean Elena."

"I'd prefer you call her Kristen."

"Why?" His tone sharpened.

Dane wasn't sure when he'd stopped thinking about her as Elena. "It keeps things simple. Less room for an avoidable slipup."

Lucian twisted a ring on his pinky. "Reasonable."

Dane's head pounded. He was in no mood for visitors. "What are you doing here?"

He didn't seem put off by Dane's gruff question. "Came by to check on the progress."

It annoyed him that Lucian expected a report. The guy worked for him and he'd left accountability behind when he'd resigned from the FBI. "There's nothing to report. It's still a waiting game."

Lucian studied him. "No signs of Benito?"

"None."

"You made contact with your man in Florida?"

"Yes. The wheels are in motion."

Lucian nodded and rose as silent as a shadow. "So you and Elena—Kristen—ate dinner? Cozy."

The muscles in his jaw tightened. "Staying close to her was part of the plan."

Lucian arched a thick, dark brow, condemnation oozing from him. "That so?"

Dane felt like a Judas…to Nancy's memory, to Lucian and to Kristen. Irritation ate at him. "If you got something to say to me, then just say it. I don't have time for a Q&A, Lucian."

"It just seems like you're getting too close to her. I wouldn't want you to lose sight of the prize."

"I haven't lost sight of anything," Dane snapped. "And isn't that the point of all this? For me to get close to her?"

Lucian's eyes darkened with an unnamed emotion. "As long as you remember she is the lure on the edge of our hook and nothing more. Catching Benito takes precedence over everything."

The idea soured his stomach. He'd never bargained on caring about—*loving*—Kristen. "I have what it takes to do the job. Now if we are finished with our little chat, I need to shower and get back to Kristen's."

He didn't like leaving her alone. Especially now.

"Do you have anything else to say before I toss you out of here?"

Lucian grinned. "Antonio Benito filed a flight plan to Virginia. He'll be here by morning."

Chapter 15

Sunday, May 20, 8:46 a.m.

"Kristen!" Sheridan's clear voice drifted through the building. Kristen, who'd been in the studio meditating in the lotus position, opened her eyes. Despite the fact that she'd only known Sheridan a couple of weeks she was happy to hear her voice.

"I'm in here." She rose and moved into the outer reception area.

Sheridan set down her bags, crossed the room to Kristen and gave her a hug. "How are you doing?"

Kristen still had not become accustomed to Sheridan's open style. "Doing well. How is the baby?"

"Gabrielle Elizabeth is doing wonderful. My sister's mother-in-law arrived last night and I decided there were too many cooks in the kitchen. I'll go back in a few weeks."

"And your sister is well?"

"Yes. She goes home tomorrow."

"I'm glad for you."

Sheridan glanced around the reception area. "So give me an update. Dane gave me his version, now I want to hear yours."

"We've been busy on getting your tearoom ready."

"We?"

"Dane. Mr. Cambia and I."

Sheridan stared at her. "You've been helping him."

Kristen wasn't going to lie to Sheridan. "He said he needed the help and was willing to pay."

"Good."

"I want you to know I got all the work done you needed done. All the winter registrants have been entered into the computer and the flyers mailed."

"I knew you would get it all done."

Kristen shook her head. "Why do you have such faith in me?"

Sheridan shrugged. "You have a pure soul. I can sense it."

Kristen didn't agree. If her soul was pure she'd have stayed in Miami and testified against her brother. She'd have tried to save Nancy Rogers. She'd done neither. Instead, she'd run like a coward. "Let me show you the room Mr. Cambia and I have been working on."

Sheridan rubbed her hands together. "I can't wait. Is it beautiful?"

"It is." She and Dane had spent yesterday afternoon painting. They'd touched a lot, kissed each other and in the late afternoon had made love again. "Mr. Cambia and I had our doubts about your color choices but they look wonderful."

Kristen opened the door. The room, painted a soft robin's-egg blue, was no longer dark and cramped. Now connected to the front room, it was twice its original size. Sunlight streamed through the bay window, glistening on the freshly painted walls. The room was cheerful.

Sheridan gasped. "It's lovelier than I ever thought it could be. You and your Mr. Cambia have done a wonderful job."

"He's not *my* Mr. Cambia."

Sheridan chuckled. "Of course, he is. I can tell by the way your eyes light up when you speak about him and the slight blush in your cheeks."

Kristen placed her hand on her cheek. "It's not what you think."

"But I sense it could be very soon."

Her intuition was always dead-on. "Why do you say this?"

"I could tell from the first moment he saw you."

"What do you mean? You weren't here when we first met."

"No, but I saw Mr. Cambia when he first saw you. You were heading out for lunch, walking on the other side of the street. The look in his eyes was very intense. As if he'd been searching for you for a long time."

Kristen shifted, uncomfortable. Dane had never mentioned anything about seeing her earlier. "He didn't tell me."

Sheridan studied the sharp neat edge of paint where trim met drywall. "Don't worry about it. He has a good soul. A warrior's heart, I think."

Unwanted seeds of doubt took root. "I suppose you are right."

Kristen didn't have time to worry about Dane. The yoga supplies Sheridan had ordered arrived and there was a good bit of unpacking to do. After an hour of work, she could see Sheridan was exhausted. The time spent at her sister's house had drained her. After much cajoling from Kristen, Sheridan agreed to go to the shelter for a nap.

Sweat trickled from her brow, and she wiped it

away. She liked working, liked having a job and making her own money. Antonio had hated the fact that she had wanted to work. He'd felt it unseemly—that people would think less of him if he allowed his sister to work. But she'd begged and pleaded. The endless hours in the stunning house by the sea had nearly driven her mad with boredom.

Finally, he'd relented and allowed her to volunteer at the library. Dignified, he'd called it. She'd only worked eight hours a week, but she'd loved it. The simple act of shelving the books, listening to the children laugh during story hour or recommending a book to someone looking for a good read.

Most women her age were out looking for real jobs and building careers. She'd wanted to be among them, but understood that as Benito's sister, her life would always be limited. But no more. She could work wherever she wished and live her life as she chose.

It wasn't until ten o'clock that she looked up and realized how late it had gotten. And that Dane hadn't arrived. His tardiness worried her. He'd been so punctual these last few days. Odd that he was late. She thought she knew him; realized she didn't.

Kristen shook off the ominous thoughts. "Borrowing trouble is your style."

Dane was late, she remembered, because he had

supplies to pick up so that he could install the shelving in the new tearoom.

The thought of Dane brought a smile to her lips. In such a short period of time, he had truly trans-formed the room, making it bright, welcoming and warm. He'd done the same to her as well. He'd drawn her out of her shell, brought her back to life.

She hefted a stock of packing boxes she'd just broken down and started out the back door to the Dumpster. She was beginning to think that maybe life was going to turn around for her.

No more hiding.

No more loneliness.

A real life.

And maybe, just maybe Dane would share his life with hers. Neither had been willing to talk about the past but in time that would come. She dragged the boxes across the alley. She slid back the door on the Dumpster and deposited the boxes inside.

She wiped her hands and turned. Halfway back to the back door she heard the sound of footsteps. Whirling around she searched the alley. She didn't see anyone. Tamping down the anxiety, she started to ease toward the studio's back door.

"Who's there?" she said. Her voice was even, firm, but her pulse galloped in her chest.

No answer.

Kristen swallowed. Her thoughts turned to Benito. Had he found her? Her mind raced through all the things she'd done in the last month. She'd been so careful not to leave any traces of her existence anywhere. But had she made a mistake?

Her pulse galloped. "Who's there?"

Seconds passed as fear clutched her belly. And then out of the shadows, she saw her. "Crystal."

The girl stood, still clutching her backpack. She looked thinner and her clothes needed cleaning. Dark circles smudged under her eyes and she could see bruises on her pale arms. Whatever anger Kristen had harbored for the girl died.

"Come inside," Kristen said.

Clearly suspicious, Crystal didn't move. "You're not mad?"

Kristen met her gaze. "I was, big-time, but I got over it."

The girl's eyes narrowed and she sniffed. She obviously didn't believe people dished out forgiveness quite so easily. "Why aren't you mad? I took your money."

Kristen laid her hand on her hip. "Cleaned me out, took every cent I had."

The girl's shoulders slumped. Instead of denial or attitude, she said, "I'm sorry."

Kristen sighed. "Is there any money left?"

Tears welled in Crystal's eyes. "No."

"What'd you use it for? Did you give it to Tony?" That would make her angry.

"No, Tony didn't know anything about the money. Rent. I used it for rent. Mom was gonna be evicted."

She had no reason to believe her, but she did. She thought about Crystal's thoughtless mother, a woman who didn't value her own child. "Come inside. You look tired."

Crystal didn't move. "You aren't going to give me the third degree or call the cops?"

"No. I can make you a meal if you are hungry." She started to walk back into the studio, not even sure if Crystal would follow.

The girl did follow, most likely out of curiosity. "Why didn't you call the cops?"

Kristen couldn't share her secrets, so she exchanged one truth for another. She closed the alley door behind her and locked it. "I know what it's like to scrape to survive, to make desperate choices. I'd like to think I'd never steal, but who's to say?"

"Yeah, but I ripped you off. My mom would have beat the crap out of me if I'd stolen one cigarette from her."

But it was okay for her child to steal rent money from someone else? Bitterness twisted inside her. "Then you better not tell her you took my money."

She started toward the stairs that led to her apartment. "I have bagels and juice if you're hungry."

"Thanks."

The girl sat down. She set her backpack beside her and accepted the bagel and juice without comment. As Kristen put a cup of water and a tea bag in the microwave, Crystal ate the first and second bagels without hardly taking a breath. She was halfway into the third when she paused. "Thanks."

After the microwave dinged, Kristen took out her green tea and sat across from the girl. She glanced at the bruise, inwardly cringing. "So, where's Tony?"

"He got arrested. But he didn't want anything to do with me since that guy chased him off."

"You mean, Dane?"

The girl's gaze snapped up and locked on hers for an instant before she dropped it back to her plate. "Yeah, that's him."

There was a hint of something in Crystal's voice that had Kristen raising her eyebrow. But she chose to let it go, chocking it up to their rocky first meeting. "So where do you go from here?"

Crystal tore a piece of bagel off but didn't eat it. "I was hoping I could stay here."

"The last time I said yes to that, I got ripped off."

"I won't steal from you again."

"Fool me once, shame on you. Fool me twice, shame on me."

"What's that supposed to mean?"

There was no anger, but hard honesty. "I don't trust you."

The girl winced, surprisingly hurt by the comment. "Right. I deserved that one."

Crystal needed someone to look after her. As tough as she appeared, she was just a kid. "Why'd you come by?"

"I was hungry. I figured you were a soft touch and you'd feed me."

Kristen sipped her tea. Her heart ached for the girl. Dane would call her a sap for what she was about to say. "I keep my money tucked in my bra now," Kristen said. "And Sheridan has all studio valuables locked in the safe. There is nothing for you to steal."

She looked very tired and fragile. "I'm not going to steal."

"Good." The downstairs door opened and she heard Dane's steady footsteps. Yesterday, she'd given him a key.

Crystal tensed. "Who's that?"

"Dane."

"What's he still doing here? I figured he'd be gone by now." The girl looked panic-stricken.

"You've nothing to be afraid of. He won't bother you as long as you don't try to steal again."

Crystal looked ready to bolt. "I don't like cops."

"Cops?" Kristen almost laughed. "Dane isn't a cop."

Crystal shook her head. "He isn't dressed like one but he acts like one. I've seen enough cops in my life to smell one a mile off. I'd bet my schoolbooks he's a cop."

Kristen's smile faded a fraction. Pieces to the Dane Cambia puzzle tumbled into place. The way he'd handled Tony. His military swagger. His stark attention to detail. His questions about her past. They all filled the cop profile. "That's ridiculous."

Dane's purposeful steps moved up the stairs toward her apartment. Involuntarily, Kristen tensed.

When he appeared at the door, he was holding a bag of groceries and wearing a smile. The instant he saw Crystal, his smile vanished. The girl's gaze skittered away.

Dane shifted his attention to her. The surprise was gone, the smile had returned. "I'm surprised you let her back in. She's a thief."

The assessing look in Dane's eyes caught Kristen short. Cop's eyes, she thought. She'd seen that look enough times when she'd been in police custody.

Crystal rose, her agitation growing. "Look, I got to get to school. I've got an exam today."

"Will you be back for supper?" Kristen said, shaking off the shadow of worry.

Crystal glanced briefly at Dane and then back at her. "Yeah. About five."

"Good."

Kristen wrapped up another couple of bagels and handed them to Crystal. The girl took the bag, glancing at Dane one last time before she hurried outside.

After he heard Crystal leave through the front door, Dane turned to her. "This is not smart."

Her defenses slammed into place. "Smart, no, but it's right."

"She's a thief."

"Yeah, well, I've done things I'm not proud of, either." She thought back to Nancy Rogers and the murdered Churchmen. She hadn't saved any of them. But maybe she could save Crystal.

He stared at her as if he had a dozen things to tell her. Instead, he nodded toward the door. "We've got a truck to unload and shelves to put up."

"Right." It felt good to shift the conversation to work. Much safer.

She followed him down the stairs and out the front door. She pushed whatever niggling thoughts she had about Dane and Crystal to the back of her mind.

He carried in a stack of two-by-fours and she

reached for a stack of molding. As she turned, something in the corner of her eye caught her attention. She looked up and saw a man standing on the street corner. Hair slicked back with dark sunglasses, he was dressed in black slacks and a cream-colored shirt. He looked so much like Benito's thug, Manuel, a man who never strayed far from her brother.

White-hot panic tightened her chest and for a moment her head swam as she stared at the car. Her heart thundered in her chest, slamming against her ribs. Her limbs started to tremble. The wood slipped from her hands and hit the ground.

Dane whirled around, his gaze razor sharp and alert. "What's wrong?"

"I saw a man." She barely had enough wind in her lungs to speak.

Dane searched the now empty street. "Who?"

She pressed trembling fingers to her temple. "A man who works for my brother!"

His gaze scanned the street block again. "There's no one on the street," he said.

She could barely breathe. "I saw him."

"What man?"

"Manuel Ortiz. He is tall. Dark hair. Has a scar on his face."

He laid his hands on her shoulders. "Whoever you saw is not there now."

"That doesn't mean he is not close."

"Why does this man scare you? And who is your brother, Kristen?"

"You don't want to know."

He laid strong hands on her shoulders. "You can trust me, Kristen."

Could she? She wasn't so sure who he was. All the unanswered questions about his past haunted her. "I know," she lied. "But it's best to let it go."

He rubbed her skin with his thumbs. "You saw a man, nothing else. Whoever this demon is from your past, it wasn't him. Don't worry about it, babe."

How could she not worry about it? She had seen Manuel Ortiz.

Later, Dane picked up his phone and called Lucian. "Benito's in town."

Chapter 16

Kristen was jumpy most of the day. Despite the fact that Dane was close she had the overwhelming fear that something was terribly wrong.

Several times she went to the window and looked out, searching for signs of Manuel. Each time, she didn't see him, but the overwhelming relief she felt was quickly eaten away by fresh worries.

Dane kept her busy running for this tool or that tool or holding the edge of a board while he cut it. But he was uncharacteristically silent. He seemed lost in his own emotions and thoughts.

His unexpected mood shift only stoked her unease

toward him, as well. When he'd fought Tony, his combat skills had been expert. He moved with military precision. When he'd seen Crystal, his eyes had reminded her of a cop's eyes.

Was Dane Cambia a cop?

As the silence stretched between them, she was reminded that she didn't know Dane Cambia at all. Since his arrival, he'd been secretive about his past, but she'd accepted that.

Now she wondered why he was so careful not to reveal anything about himself. By midafternoon, she realized she had to get out of the house. She needed perspective or her fears were going to drive her insane. She thought about Sheridan. Sheridan was level-headed and her intuition was always so dead-on. Perhaps Sheridan could help her put perspective on her emotions and worries.

"Dane," she said as she closed up a can of blue paint. "I've got to run to the youth shelter to see Sheridan. I forgot that we've got to go over registrations. There is a problem that can't wait. I should be back in a half hour or so."

He glanced up from a fresh can he'd just opened. "I'll drive you."

She thought about Manuel. There'd been no sign of him since her first glimpse. She would run the few blocks to the youth shelter. "It's only three blocks and the walk will do me good. And if I go now, I'll be back by the time you're finished. We can have supper together." She'd added the last bit to dispel the worry in his eyes.

It didn't seem to work. "Okay."

She managed a bright smile as she leaned over and kissed him on the lips. "See you soon."

He captured her arm and held her close for a moment. "Hurry back." And he kissed her again, as if he couldn't get enough of her, and then reluctantly released her.

"I will." Kristen dashed upstairs and grabbed her knapsack and was out the front door in seconds. The air was cool and the sun bright.

On the street, she passed an old woman who nodded a greeting. A gentle breeze blew through her hair as she crossed an intersection. Her mouth felt dry and her back tight with tension. She found herself searching for Manuel's tall muscular frame, dark hair and black eyes. Sweat trickled down her spine.

But she didn't see him. And with each new step, her worries faded a little. Manuel and Benito were in Florida, she reminded herself. She'd been so careful to cover all her tracks. He couldn't possibly have found her.

In the clear light of day under an azure sky, she began to wonder if she'd overreacted to her supposed sighting of Manuel and to Crystal's insistence that Dane was a cop. She was so used to trouble; she now seemed to see it everywhere.

Shoving out a breath, she forced herself to inhale deeply. The shelter was only a block away now. She would tell her friend the truth about herself, listen to her words of wisdom and put her worries behind her. Yes, Sheridan would tell her she was being silly and not to worry.

Kristen refused to give in to fear or let her brother rob her of another moment's happiness.

As she reached the next intersection, she noticed a man crossing the street toward her. He was wearing a Grateful Dead T-shirt, had bound his shoulder-length hair with a piece of rawhide and wore a gold looped earring in his left ear. He looked out of place.

The man smiled at her. "Excuse me, I think I'm lost."

Kristen tightened her hold on her bag. "Really? Where are you headed?"

He stopped beside her, just a foot away. He stood over six feet and she had to tip her head back to meet his gaze. Dark glasses shaded his eyes. "The courthouse."

She noted the large signet ring on his left index finger. "It's three blocks to the north."

"North? Is that left or right?" His grin was sheepish, charming.

She smiled and pointed toward a redbrick townhouse that was under renovation. "Just head that way."

He pulled off his glasses. "Thanks."

When her gaze locked with his, her breath caught in her throat. She saw the eyes of the last man Antonio had killed. The old man who'd spit on her brother's shoes.

Kristen felt dizzy and stepped back. Those last terrible moments in the warehouse crashed in around her. Her heart hammered in her chest.

The stranger's eyes narrowed. "You okay?"

She nodded weakly. "I'm fine." Every fear she'd tried to tuck away broke free. There were just too many coincidences today. "I've got to go."

His body had tensed, but he made no move to stop her. "Have a nice day."

She didn't bother to answer as she started to run now to Sheridan's. To her great relief the man didn't follow. Ignoring the burn of unshed tears in her throat, she glanced from side to side and crossed the last intersection. Sheridan's was only a block away.

She'd just stepped up on the curb when she heard, "Elena."

For a moment, she thought what she'd heard had been a trick of the mind.

"Elena!"

She stopped and turned.

Antonio's Mercedes was parked behind her. Standing beside the car was Manuel. He wore sunglasses, an expensive gray suit.

If he was here, then so was Benito.

She turned to run but collided with another tall, muscular, faceless man dressed in black. He grabbed her by the arm and started dragging her toward the car.

Antonio had found her.

Dane had followed Kristen when she'd left for the youth shelter.

She'd said she'd seen Manuel Ortiz and though he'd downplayed the incident, he knew she'd seen Benito's right-hand man. She was scared.

But it was more than fear of her brother that ate at her. She didn't trust him. Something had changed between them. Otherwise she wouldn't have taken her knapsack.

Dane wanted to stay behind Kristen but knew if she saw him following, she'd bolt. So he'd called Lucian immediately and told him to keep an eye on her.

As he headed down a parallel side street toward the shelter, he heard a woman scream. He knew it was Kristen. His blood ran cold. Dane drew the .32 from his ankle holster and dashed down the alleyway toward her. When he reached Sheridan's street he saw Lucian, gun drawn and pointed at a large gorilla of a man who held Kristen by her hair and poked a gun in her side. They were in the middle of the street and the man was dragging Kristen toward a black Mercedes.

Cold rage washed over Dane.

He wanted to fire at the goon but didn't want to risk hitting Kristen.

She drew back her elbow and rammed it into the gorilla's gut. The man grunted, yanked hard on her hair, making her scream again. She dug in her heels and tried to reach behind her head and scratch his hands.

Lucian raised his gun.

"Stop," Dane ordered Lucian. "I don't want her hurt."

At the sound of Dane's voice, Kristen's head jerked toward him. Confusion, fear and anger crossed her tense features, as if her worst suspicion had been confirmed.

The gorilla tightened his hold on Kristen. "Stay out of this matter," he shouted. "This is family business."

Dane aimed his gun at the gorilla's head. "Let her go."

The man growled his anger. Another man got out of the Mercedes and shouted an order in Spanish. The gorilla started to drag Kristen toward the car.

Dane moved into the center of the street, his gun pointed at the man's head. Lucian was to his right, his gun also pointed at the man. Dane knew if the man got Kristen in the car he might never see her again. He wasn't thinking about catching Benito but of saving her.

He aimed for the man standing beside the Mercedes and fired.

The man by the car grabbed his chest and stumbled back against the car.

The gorilla was distracted for just a moment and looked back at his comrade. Dane fired again. This bullet flew dangerously close to Kristen's face, striking the gorilla in the arm. The man stumbled back. The force of the shot was enough to make him relax his hold on Kristen. Taking advantage, she jerked free and stumbled away from the car.

Realizing she was out of his reach, the gorilla jumped in the car and slammed the door seconds before it sped off.

Lucian started to run after the car. He fired his gun at the back windshield. The bullets skidded off bulletproof glass.

"Let it go, Lucian," Dane shouted. "Benito's not in the car."

At the mention of her brother's name, Kristen stopped and looked up at Dane. Dark smudges of mascara darkened the skin under her eyes and her face was as pale as the moon. What tore at his gut, however, was the utter look of horror as she stared at him.

He reached out to her. "Let's get out of here, Kristen."

She stepped back, glancing at Lucian and then back at him. "How did you know my brother's name?"

"This is not the place," Dane said, reaching for her again.

She slapped his hand away. "I knew something was wrong but I didn't want to believe it. You have cop eyes."

He tried to take her hand. "I have your best interests at heart."

She flinched and moved out of his reach. "Don't touch me."

Pain twisted his heart. He'd shattered Kristen's fragile trust and for that he would never forgive himself. But what mattered most now was keeping Kristen safe. And in the open street, she was not safe.

He grabbed her by the arm. "We need to get out of here."

Lucian reloaded his gun as he approached. "I don't see anyone else now. But we've got to go."

Kristen's gaze darted between the two. "I'm not going anywhere with either of you."

"It's either me or your brother," Dane said.

She backed away a step. "How do I know you don't work for him? There is a hefty bounty on my head. Maybe you want to sell me to my brother and cheat Manuel out of the reward money."

"This is not the place for this," Lucian said through clenched teeth. He scanned the streets again for any sign of Benito's men.

"Both of you can go to hell," she said.

In the distance, Dane heard a police siren. Someone had seen what had happened or heard the shots fired. Dane knew Benito owned many on the police force. Kristen would not be safe with them. He was the only one that could save her now.

He holstered his gun and moving with lightning speed, shoved his shoulder into her belly. He picked her up as Lucian ran to his Suburban parked across the street and opened the back door.

Kristen pounded his back with her fists and kicked her feet into his stomach. "Leave me alone, you bastard. I'm not going back! I'm not going back to my brother! I would rather die first."

Dane dumped her in the back of the Suburban and shoved her to the center. She scrambled to the other door, tried the handle and discovered it was locked. Grim satisfaction burned in him as he closed the door behind him. She was safe.

Lucian slid behind the wheel and within seconds

they were moving through the town's streets and toward the mountain highway.

Kristen started to pound on the tinted window. "You can't do this to me!"

Lucian kept his eyes on the road. He held the steering wheel in a white-knuckle grip. "The glass is shatter and soundproof."

"It's all right, Kristen," Dane said. "We do not work for your brother." Dane laid his hand on her shoulder, trying to calm her.

She flinched and slapped it away. "Don't touch me!"

He curled his fingers as if burned and drew them away. "You're only going to hurt yourself hitting the glass."

His calmly spoken words didn't reach her right away. But as seconds passed and her hands grew sore from hitting the glass, she stopped her struggles. Her eyes were full of rage and fear as she looked at him.

The rage he could handle, but not the fear. If he could have handled this any other way, he would have. "Let me explain."

Tears streamed down her face. "You lied to me."

"I had to."

She shook her head. "I don't want to hear anything you have to say, ever again."

Chapter 17

Kristen's mind was numb as Lucian's car sped down country roads. She didn't bother to plead or beg for her release. One look at Dane's stony face told her she'd be wasting her time.

How could she have been such a fool? How could she have believed that she could ever have a real life? As Antonio Benito's sister, her existence would forever be different from everyone else's.

She wished a thousand curses on Dane's soul because he'd let her believe again in happy endings, something she was destined never to have. Her world would forever be dark, dangerous, loveless. Her heart shattered at the thought.

As the car drove down the street, she started to regroup. She'd become an expert at improvising. Pushing aside the pieces of her broken heart, she began to plan. She would not roll over and give up, not even for Dane Cambia. She was a survivor, she reminded herself. Happiness may not be her destiny but no matter what it took, she would get away from Dane and her brother.

When the car finally came to a stop, her body went on alert. There'd be no escaping while the car was moving but she had a slim chance of getting away now.

She tensed, ready to bolt at the first opportunity.

Dane wrapped long, strong fingers around her arm and pulled her toward him. "We're at the safe house."

Ignoring the softness in his voice, she didn't resist his steel grip. "Where are we going?"

"Where I can protect you."

She did not want his protection. She wanted nothing from him. But she kept those thoughts to herself and slid out his door. Bright sunlight had her wincing. She tossed a glance at Lucian, who seemed totally unconcerned about her anger and fear.

Kristen focused on Dane. "If you aren't going to sell me to my brother then why am I here?"

"Inside," Lucian said.

Inside. She glanced at the rugged cabin. At first glance it looked like any other mountain cabin, but a closer inspection revealed tinted windows and extra locks on the front door, which she suspected were reinforced. The place was a fortress.

Dane and Lucian had been planning this for a while, and the thought sent terror through her body. If they got her inside that cabin, she would be completely trapped. She glanced toward the door, not twenty feet away, and then cut her gaze to the right toward a stand of trees. The trees were a good one hundred feet away. But in the woods, she could hide.

Lucian moved ahead, pulled a ring of keys out of his pocket and unlocked the door.

She needed to throw Dane and Lucian off balance, make them hesitate so she could get away. "You lied to me. You made love to me. You betrayed me."

The words hit their mark. A flicker of pain darkened Dane's eyes. "I've got good reason. And when this is all over, I can only hope you understand why I did what I did."

He'd dropped the southern accent. The soft jovial look in his face was gone, as well. She didn't know him at all. "I will never understand what you did."

He stared stonily at her for several long seconds. Then with grim resolve started to pull her toward the house. She let herself be taken the first few steps, expecting he'd lower his guard because he had her. She curled her fingers into a white-knuckled fist. She'd only have one shot so she needed to make it good.

She drew back her fist and punched Dane right in the eye.

The explosion of pain had him wincing and for a brief second, he slackened his hold on her arm. That's all she needed.

She jerked her arm free and started to run.

"Damn," he muttered.

She saw woods up ahead and sensed if she could make the stand of trees she had a chance of escaping. She heard Lucian shout, heard the thunder of Dane's feet behind her.

Her heart slammed in her chest. The woods. Just get to the woods. There she could hide or get lost in the thick underbrush.

Footsteps pounded hard behind her. She could feel their vibration in the earth.

She was only feet from the first stand of trees when she felt his hands on her. He tackled her. At the last second, he twisted his body so that he absorbed the brunt of the fall. She landed on his chest. The wind whooshed out of her body and for a moment she was too stunned to move.

Her chance of escape had vanished.

She was trapped.

Something inside of her snapped.

"Let go of me!" She screamed and pounded on his chest. She'd make as much noise as her vocal cords could summon. "Help! Help!"

Dane captured her hands at her side. "No one can hear you, Kristen."

Kristen fought Dane as if she were possessed.

Clenching her fist, she drove it into his ribs, letting years of anger and frustration ricochet through her body.

Dane grunted in pain and muttered an oath. As she drew up her knee ready to drive it into his groin, he rolled her on her back and captured her hands in his and pinned them to the ground. His body trapped her against the ground so that she couldn't draw up her knees.

"Stop," he hissed against her ear.

"Get off me!" Her voice cracked and it took everything in her not to cry. She'd never felt more betrayed. More alone.

Dane's heart thundered hard and fast against her chest. His face was right above hers. "I can't do that."

She spit in his face.

Cursing, he jerked his body up and pulled her with him. As he wiped the spittle from his face, the raw intensity in his eyes took her breath away. Antonio had looked at other men like that and they had all died. But Dane kept his anger under tight control.

Provoking Dane was not productive and Kristen drew in a breath, forcing her anger deep inside her. It was a talent she'd mastered in Benito's house—one that had enabled her to survive. And no matter what, she would find a way to survive this.

"Are you a cop?" she demanded.

"Yes."

"Antonio has proven that he will never let me testify."

Dane ground his teeth. "I'm not interested in going through the court system again."

That brought her up short. "Then why all this?"

"Inside first." His grip on her arm tightened.

As they approached the cabin's front door her bravado waned. "Who are you?" she demanded.

Dane jerked the front door open and dragged her inside. She tripped over a small carpet by the front door and would have fallen if his grip hadn't remained firm.

The interior of the cabin was dim. As her eyes adjusted from the bright sunlight, she could see that it was simply furnished with a crate-style couch and matching chairs, an empty coffee table and three end tables with cheap lights. No carpet adorned the floor and simple white pull-down shades covered the windows. There was a kitchen off to the right, doors that must lead to bedrooms or bathrooms. Practical and functional.

She heard movement coming from the kitchen and assumed it was the other man—the driver. What had Dane called him? Lucian.

"Sit down," Dane ordered as he pulled her toward a chair.

"Tell me what you want. I am sick of games."

Dane shoved her in the chair. "This is no game."

"No bounty. No court. Why am I here?"

Lucian walked into the room. "You are the bait for the trap."

Her gaze shifted from Dane to Lucian and back. "What trap?"

"We want Benito," Dane said.

Kristen noted the clenched fists at Dane's side—remembered how tenderly he'd stroked her hair with them. Agony squeezed her heart. "What do you want him for?"

"The Churchmen murders," Lucian said.

Mention of the murders knocked the wind from her. The night of those vicious murders twisted her soul. The screams of the men filled her ears.

"My uncle was one of the men murdered that night," Lucian said. Despite the stony look on his face, raw pain dripped from his words.

Kristen looked at Lucian. She remembered each of the faces of the men Antonio had murdered. They were imprinted on her soul. Now she understood why Lucian had the eyes of the last man murdered.

As she remembered the old man with pride and anger, the fight in her vanished. A sudden, unexpected tear escaped down her cheek. "Were you close to your uncle?"

Lucian understood. "He raised me like his own."

"I am sorry," she said.

The softly spoken words caught him off guard before he recovered his composure. "I don't want your pity," Lucian snapped. "You had the chance to put your brother away and you didn't."

She lifted her chin. "I went to the police. I tried to help. The police couldn't protect me."

"My sister died trying to protect you," Dane said. Rage coated each word.

Her gaze speared Dane. "Nancy," she said softly. "Your sister was Nancy Rogers?"

Hearing his sister's name from her lips clearly shocked him. "You remember her?"

"Not a day goes by when I don't think about Nancy or the men shot in that warehouse." She shifted her gaze to Lucian. "I remember your uncle. You have his eyes. He was brave to the very last moment."

Pain darkened Lucian's eyes.

"He spat on Antonio's shoes," she added.

Grim satisfaction eased the lines on his face before he turned, overcome with emotion, and left the room.

She watched Lucian leave before turning back to Dane. "I say a prayer for Nancy and those men every night," she said softly. Tears spilled down her cheeks. "She ordered me to leave."

The muscle in his jaw tensed. "Don't."

"What? Make you feel pain?" she challenged. She swiped away the tear. "You sliced a knife through my heart." She shook her head, coming to a heinous realization. "My brother hurt you, so you decided to hurt me as revenge."

He shook his head. "What happened between us had nothing to do with this."

Her laugh was bitter. "I am not a fool. You saw the opportunity to strike a blow at the Benito family and you took it."

"It wasn't like that," he ground out.

"So why didn't you reveal yourself to me at first? Why the games?" She folded her arms over her chest, needing the protection.

"We needed to confirm your ID."

"And after that?" she challenged. "You made love to me under the pretext of a lie."

"What happened between us in bed was not a lie."

She held up her hand, silencing him. His treachery nearly tore her in half. "You told Benito where I am, didn't you?"

"Yes."

"You bastard."

He didn't argue.

"You might as well have put a bullet in my head now, because Antonio will see to it that I wish for death for the rest of my life."

Resolve flattened his lips into a grim line. "I won't let him get you."

"Your arrogance is touching, Dane, but naive. Your name is Dane, isn't it?"

The tart edge to her voice had him tensing his jaw. "That's my name."

A sprinkle of truth among the lies—he was a clever man. "Antonio is stronger than you are. No one can defeat him."

"I will."

Despite all that he'd done, she did not want to see him hurt. "You are a fool to believe this."

He reached out to touch her.

She flinched, unable to bear his touch again. It was too painful. "Don't ever touch me again."

"Kristen. Elena…"

The sound of her given name made her cringe. "Don't call me Elena. Elena died nine months ago. And thanks to you, Kristen will be dead soon enough."

He shoved his hands in his pocket. "I won't let him touch you."

"You won't be able to stop him. The entire Miami police force couldn't stop him. He will crush you."

He paced the floor. "Kristen. When this is over…"

"We will both be dead." She drew her shoulders back. Her days of cowering were over. "Is there some other room where I can stay? Lock me in it if you must, but I can't bear to look at you anymore."

He nodded to the door to her right. "That's a bedroom."

"Fine."

He followed her to the room and opened the door. "The windows are bolted shut. And an alarm will sound if you break the panes."

"So efficient."

He stared at her, pain etched in his rawboned features.

She slammed the door in his face.

Dane felt horrible.

He collapsed on the couch and dropped his head back against the cushions. He wasn't sure how much time passed before he heard the front door open. He whirled around, gun drawn. It was Lucian.

"If you can't go through with this," Lucian said. He'd tightly reined in his emotions again. "I will finish it."

Dane sat up. "I'll see this through."

Lucian studied him, his hooded gaze as emotionless as the computers he loved. "It's no longer black and white for you."

He hated Benito. He loved Kristen. But everything else in between was a muddled, gray mess. "I want Benito dead."

"And you want his sister."

"Yes."

Lucian muttered an oath.

"You sure can pick 'em, Cambia," Lucian said.

Dane couldn't summon an argument.

Still, who Kristen was didn't change the way he felt about her. If not for all this mess, Dane and Kristen could have been happy. He'd not realized until now how the promise of happiness had tantalized him, given him a sense of hope.

He wanted Kristen. Wanted the promise of what they could have had. And he would find a way to get through to her. He would convince her that he'd made love to her because he couldn't keep his hands off her. That those feelings had nothing to do with Benito.

Dane laid his head back against the cushion. He'd

only closed his eyes a moment when he heard the crash and an alarm sounded.

"Damn!" Lucian shouted. He was already racing to Kristen's door. "She's smashed the window."

Kristen glanced back at the chair wedged under the doorknob as she lifted a second chair and drove it through the half-shattered window. A screeching alarm blared in her ears. The wood splintered and cracked and the final blow shattered it completely. Satisfied she could crawl through it, she grabbed the bedspread puddled by the window and laid it over the jagged glass edges.

She heard the lock turn in the door.

"Kristen!" Dane shouted. He crashed against the door, likely driving his shoulder into the wood. The old wood cracked but didn't give way. But it would soon.

She only had seconds.

Saying a prayer of mercy, she climbed over the bedspread, wincing as a shard of glass cut into her knee. She swallowed the pain, knowing it would pass and was worth the price of freedom. She fell forward and tumbled to the ground five feet below. She hit the ground hard, wincing as her cut knee ground into the dirt.

She scrambled to her feet, again her eyes to the woods. To freedom.

"Kristen!" Dane shouted.

She made the mistake of glancing back just as Dane stared down at her. She scrambled to her feet. Her pants were torn, her knee sliced by the glass. Pain burned and she could feel warm blood rushing down her leg. But she ran.

She heard him vault out the window and run toward her. She made it fifteen feet before strong hands were on top of her shoulders, pulling her back.

Pain and frustration collided when he touched her. Her composure shattered.

"Let me go!" she screamed.

Dane wrapped his arms around her waist, pulled her back against his chest. "Jesus, Kristen, what have you done to yourself? You're bleeding."

She saw the blood streaming down her leg but didn't care. "Let go of me!"

"I can't." His voice cracked and the emotion she heard destroyed her. "I can't."

She started to weep. "Let go of me. You are the devil. Worse than Antonio."

He turned her around lifted her into his arms. Her blood smeared his shirt, his face. But he didn't release her.

"I beg you, please let me go." The fight drained from her body.

"I can't." He lifted her into his arms and carried

her inside and laid her on the couch. Her senses were on overload. She couldn't think. Coherent thought had abandoned her.

She was aware of Lucian handing Dane a first-aid kit.

"It's fully equipped," Lucian said.

Dane pushed up the leg of her jeans. "She's going to need stitches."

"Don't touch me, either of you." She slapped their hands away as they tried to inspect the cut.

"I've got a tranquillizer." Lucian prepared a needle and she started to scream in earnest.

"No! No drugs." The pain in her leg was growing worse.

"Kristen, I've got to stitch you up. It will be better if you are asleep," Dane said.

"Devil. You are the devil."

The needle pricked her arm and in the next moments she started to feel herself floating.

The pain vanished.

And so did the concerned faces of the men staring down at her.

Kristen dreamed of devils, hands reaching up from the underworld trying to pull her down to hell.

A part of her wanted to surrender to the demons and let them take her. She was so tired of fighting.

But deep in her core there was a drive that would not allow her to surrender.

So, she fought, flaying her arms, kicking. She wanted to live. Wanted to have a normal life away from the violence. And then out of the darkness, strong arms took ahold of her, pulling her into a warm, strong embrace.

"Shh," a voice soothed. "It's all right. I'm here for you. I won't ever leave you."

The rich, deep voice calmed her nerves and soothed her fears. Strong arms cradled her. She knew she shouldn't trust. Trust equaled danger. But she wanted to feel protected so badly. If only for a few minutes, she wanted to feel safe and loved.

So she relaxed into the embrace, praying that tomorrow she'd have the strength to run.

When Kristen awoke, her brain was groggy and her reflexes slow. For a moment, she didn't know where she was or what had happened.

Laying on her side, her arm brushed against hard muscle and she realized wherever she was, she was not alone.

She blinked, focused, turned her head. Dane. His eyes were closed, his hand draped over her waist. His scent enveloped her.

Her eyes closed again. Groggy, she smiled. Lord,

but she loved it when he touched her. She rolled on her back, savoring the delicious warmth of his body. She stared at his proud, lean face and knew that she loved him.

She tried to sit up but when she bent her knee, pain rocketed up her leg. She glanced down and saw the bandage. *What had happened to her?*

Worry started to chip away at the contentment that had been so complete moments ago. What had happened to her? She scrambled to remember. Through the haze, her memory tumbled into place like pieces of a puzzle. The tension in her body grew.

And then the picture was complete.

Dane had betrayed her.

The sense of loss was as fresh as if it had just happened.

She started to shift out of his hold.

"You're awake," Dane said. He was fully alert.

"Let go of me."

He slowly withdrew his arm, letting his fingers brush her skin. "Take it easy with the leg. You've got seven stitches."

She struggled to sit up, careful to keep her leg straight. Looking around the room, she saw the window she'd smashed had been boarded up. Her blood, which had stained the floor, had been cleaned.

But she was still trapped in this house.

"How long have I been out?" she said.

"Twelve hours."

Twelve hours. "Sheridan will wonder where I am."

"I called her. Told her we were going on a date."

Resentment twisted her heart. "You've thought of everything."

He didn't answer.

Kristen shoved trembling hands through her hair and eased her leg over the side. It burned as if a poker had scorched her skin.

Dane sat up, his lips a flat grim line. Dark stubble blanketed his square jaw. "I can get you something for the pain."

"No more drugs."

"It will help."

"Antonio tried to control me with drugs when I was a teenager. No drugs."

"When did he do this?" Anger coated each word.

"It was after my parents died. I was crying a lot, so he started putting tranquilizers in my food. For almost a year, I wandered around in a haze before he weaned me off the drugs."

He scowled as he listened. "All right. No more drugs."

She wouldn't beg him again to let her go. There was no point wasting her breath.

Dane's wide shoulders rose and fell as he shoved out a breath. "I want to explain."

"Explain why you lied to me?"

"Explain why I set this whole thing in motion."

She thought about his sister Nancy. Nancy. "If you had come to me as who you are, I might have helped you."

"You would have helped?" His doubt was clear.

She glanced at his dark, stern eyes filled with emotion and then looked away. "I would have." It would have been her chance to avenge Nancy.

"I couldn't take the chance that you wouldn't help."

Being this close to him was so hard. Even after all that had happened she wanted him to take her in his arms and hold her close.

Needing distance, she rose and limped to the door. She tried the knob. It was locked. "Now you can take a chance on me. I will help you catch my brother."

He rose up off the bed. "Are you sure about this?"

"Never more sure." The time to stop running had arrived.

Dane took a step toward her.

She held up her hand to stop him. "But know that when this is over, I want nothing to do with you again."

Chapter 18

Monday, May 21, 7:26 a.m.

The phone call came as Dane and Kristen stepped into the living room. Lucian looked up from the papers he was reading, which were splayed across the kitchen table.

Dane glanced at Kristen and then the number, and not recognizing it, flipped open the phone. "Cambia."

"Mr. Cambia, you are quite a resourceful man." Benito's voice rang clear.

His gut tightened. He motioned to Kristen and Lucian, signaling it was Benito. "That so?"

Kristen tensed and folded her arms over her chest.

Immediately, Lucian went to his computer and started to trace the call.

"I have been looking for Elena for over a year and you and your friend Mr. Moss find her in under a week," Benito said smoothly. "I am impressed and grateful."

Dane held Kristen's gaze. She wanted in on the capture of her brother and he wasn't going to hide anything else from her. No more secrets between them ever again. "If you want her, she's gonna cost you."

Unflinching, Kristen held his gaze.

"Ah," Benito crooned. "Nothing in life is free, is it, Mr. Cambia. How much do you want?"

Lucian clenched and unclenched his fingers. The rage had deepened the lines on his face.

"Ten million," Cambia said.

"A lot of money for a woman." Anger had stripped the silk from his voice.

Dane wanted to take Kristen in his arms. She deserved so much better than her brother, and yes, him.

Lucian studied his computer screen. He held up two fingers. He needed two more minutes to trace the call.

Dane needed to stretch the call out as long as he could. "If you want her back, then it's going to cost you ten million."

"And if I don't pay?" Benito said.

"I put a bullet in her brain."

Kristen dropped her gaze.

Saying the words in front of her made him feel as slimy as the man he was hunting. He prayed one day Kristen could forgive him. That he could forgive himself.

Dane could hear Benito taking a drag off of one of his signature Cuban cigars and then blowing out the smoke. He wasn't thrown off by any of this. "I have a counteroffer, Mr. Cambia."

Dane checked his watch. A minute thirty seconds to go. "I'm willing to hear what you have to say."

Benito's chuckle was filled with genuine mirth. Likely he knew Dane was trying to draw out the conversation. "We shall see. Have a listen."

A young girl screamed. It was clear she was terrified.

Dane's gaze locked with Lucian's. He motioned for him to hurry his tracing program any way he could. Lucian shook his head, indicating he could not.

"Who is that?" Dane said. "What kind of game are you playing?"

"I have Elena's little friend. Crystal is her name, I believe." He sighed. "Elena was always fond of strays. Always begging me to let her keep this kitten, that puppy. Of course, I always said no. You never know what kinds of diseases the little scoundrels have."

Dane's mind reeled. Crystal was an angle he hadn't considered. If he was going to save the girl he had to remain calm. "The girl means nothing to me."

Kristen's eyes narrowed when her gaze met his. Lucian started to walk toward her, motioning for her to be silent.

"Ah, but I hear otherwise," Benito said. "The girl says she is a friend of Elena's. She also tells me that you and my sister are quite close."

Dane gripped the phone. "This transaction is only about the money as far as I'm concerned."

"Strictly business," Benito teased.

"Yes."

"As a businessman you must appreciate that I must try to get the best price that I can."

"What are you proposing?" It took extra effort for Dane to keep his voice even.

"I let Crystal keep her fingers and toes and you give me my sister. And because I am feeling generous, I will let you live."

"What about the money?"

Benito laughed. "Dead men cannot spend money, Mr. Cambia."

Kristen's face had grown deadly pale. "And if I don't deal."

"I kill the girl and then I come after you and your friend, Mr. Moss."

The goal wasn't to get the money. The goal was to capture Benito. But if he relented on the money too easily, Benito would sniff a trap. "Toss in five million and you have a deal. And whatever you do to the girl I do to Kristen."

Kristen swallowed. The panic in her eyes twisted his gut.

Benito laughed. "You don't bluff very well, Mr. Cambia."

Dane drew in a breath and then hung up the phone.

Kristen's eyes widened with alarm. "What are you doing?"

"It is a calculated risk," he said. "If I am going to save Crystal, I have to play hardball."

Tears filled Kristen's eyes. "He has Crystal."

He nodded tersely. "Yes."

She turned her face away from his so he didn't see the tears fall.

Dane moved toward her when Lucian's words stopped him. "Benito's local—in the state—but you hung up too soon to get a hard fix on him. Why did you hang up?"

"He knew there was a tap on the line. He'd have hung up before the two minutes. This is the only way to keep him on the hook."

Kristen pressed a trembling hand to her temple. "Crystal is just a child. This is not her fight."

"I will get her back." Dane never made promises lightly. He would move heaven and earth to make this right.

Anger brightened her brown eyes. "He will take his anger out on Crystal."

Dane believed he'd made the right move. "I don't think so. I think he wants you back *very* badly. I think he is the one who is bluffing. He doesn't want you hurt."

"He will kill her," Kristen said.

"Not right away. Not until he knows he has you back safe and sound."

Lucian cocked an eyebrow. "And if you are wrong?"

Kristen moved to the couch and sat down. Her eyes were bright with worry. "I should never have befriended her, but I felt sorry for her."

Dane sat next to her, still careful not to touch. "I will get her back."

"Your promises mean nothing to me."

Dane was glad for her anger. He could handle it far better than he could the wounded look of betrayal in her eyes. Anger also signified that she still had fight left in her and she was going to need every ounce of it to get through this. "They will once this is over."

"So what do we do?" Lucian said. He folded his arms over his chest.

"We wait for him to call," Dane said.

Lucian shoved his hands in his pockets. "We *wait!* What makes you think he will call?" His voice was louder now, angry.

Instinct. It had gotten him through many undercover operations. "He will."

Lucian shook his head. "I deal in facts, figures and computer programs. There I can control the variables, the outcome. I make educated guesses that pay off ninety-eight-point-seven percent of the time. You are dealing with an animal. And animals are unpredictable. You don't have a damn idea what that bastard is going to do."

"He will call," Kristen said softly.

Both men looked at her.

"Dane is right. My brother wants me back in his house. And he will do whatever it takes."

"Why does he want you so much?" Dane said. That question had plagued him since the beginning. Several sick and twisted scenarios had played in his mind that he hadn't dared voice.

Kristen straightened her shoulders. "Antonio is a very superstitious man. He dabbles in the occult and has a team of seers and fortune-tellers who advise him on what to do each day. He believes they have kept him alive this long." She picked at the edge of the white bandage neatly wrapped around her knee. "Antonio believes I bring him luck."

"That's it?" Lucian said. "You are his lucky charm?"

"In his mind, it's more complicated than that. He believes I am his muse, his guardian against evil. Without my purity to guard him, he believes the forces of evil will devour him."

"That's insane," Dane said.

"My brother is insane. Many times he was quite psychotic."

"That's why he kept you locked in his house."

"Yes. He didn't want me to leave, fearing the evil would destroy him."

"Why were you with him the night of the murders?" Lucian said.

"I had tried to leave my brother. I was in love and wanted to run away and marry. Antonio caught me trying to leave. He wanted to teach me a lesson."

Lucian crossed the room toward Kristen. "Murdering my uncle was just one of his lessons?" Fury dissolved into disbelief and pain.

Kristen met his gaze. "I'm afraid so. He was quite angry with your uncle for interfering with his drug trade. He wanted to set an example."

Lucian crumbled into a seat beside Kristen. "Six good men. Dead because of one crazy, greedy bastard."

Kristen laid her hand on Lucian's shoulder. "I

begged for his life, for the lives of his friends. I could not save them and that will haunt me for the rest of my days."

Lucian swallowed. Strong emotions made it impossible for him to speak.

Dane's cell phone rang, and all three of them froze. It rang a second time.

"Answer it!" Lucian said.

Dane held up a finger and waited for the third ring before he flipped it open. "Cambia."

"Mr. Cambia, you drive a very hard bargain," Benito said.

"I'm a stubborn bastard," Dane said. "Don't ever forget that."

"I want my Elena," Benito said. For the first time, Dane heard a hint of desperation.

"So what are you willing to do for me?" Dane could not show weakness now.

"I will pay you one million dollars and give you the girl."

A smile tipped the edge of Dane's lips. He had him. "Make it two million."

"Don't push me," Benito warned. "I am being very generous."

"I wouldn't push your luck, Benito. Without Elena, you are quite vulnerable, aren't you?" He thought about the money that Lucian had stolen from all Benito's computer-based businesses. "How much of your business has been stripped clean since she vanished?"

Silence was his only answer for five long seconds and then, "You have a deal."

"There's an abandoned amusement park outside of town. Appletown. Meet me there in two hours."

Benito was silent for a long moment. "Agreed. But I will expect you there in one hour."

"I'll need two."

"One or no deal."

Dane sensed he'd pushed Benito to the breaking point. "Deal."

Benito hung up.

"He is drawing you into a trap." The worry in Kristen's voice gave him a measure of hope. Whether she liked it or not, she cared about him. Maybe after all this she could forgive him.

"I would expect nothing less."

Dane's cell phone rang again. Surprised, he flipped it open. "Cambia."

"Mr. Cambia, this is Sheridan Taylor." Steel coated each word. "I want to know where Kristen and Crystal are."

"They're just fine."

"Really? Then why did I find Kristen's backpack outside the shelter?"

He had no quick answer for that. "Would you like me to put her on the phone?"

"No. I want to see that she is fine with my own two eyes. Have her at the studio in twenty minutes or I am calling the cops."

Chapter 19

Dane drove the Suburban into town. Lucian sat at his right. Kristen was in the backseat.

She was scared.

She'd not seen Benito in over a year and she knew that if he got ahold of her, she would never see the light of day. She'd be his pet forever. But the alternative was to run and live the life of a coward. And she'd had enough of that.

Dane had not spoken to her in the last half hour. And she was glad. Her emotions were so raw she didn't trust her reaction.

The car slowed and turned onto Elm Street where

the yoga studio was located. She shifted in her seat and pulled back her shoulders. Her knee had started to ache and she couldn't move fast with the stitches in place. But mental quickness was what she needed now. She had to outsmart Benito.

Dane parked the Suburban in front of the yoga studio. The front door opened. Sheridan.

"You've got to convince her you are okay," Lucian said.

Kristen nodded. "I'll try."

Dane shut off the engine. "You've got to do more than try unless you want to risk her life."

Kristen didn't argue. She opened her door and gingerly got out of the car. Closing the door, she limped forward a step.

Dane hurried around the car and cupped his hand under her elbow.

Immediately, she flinched and tried to pull away. "I can walk on my own."

"You've got seven stitches in your knee. And there's no time to put you back together again if you bust one."

She tightened her jaw, hating his logic. With his help, she limped toward the steps. It was slow going up the stairs to the front door because she had to keep her knee straight. And she realized she wouldn't have made it if not for Dane. When they reached the top step, he released her.

Kristen pushed her hand through her hair. "Sheridan."

Sheridan hugged Kristen. "I was so worried about you."

"I had a little accident." She nodded to her knee. "I took a tumble, needed to get a few stitches, but I am fine now. I just need to get some rest."

"I'll keep an eye on her," Dane offered.

A thousand unspoken questions flashed in Sheridan's pale blue eyes as she glared at Dane. But before she could respond, police lights flashed and a squad car pulled up in front of the studio. Kristen tensed.

Sheridan nodded, satisfied. "I called them fifteen minutes ago. I didn't trust Mr. Cambia here. I thought you were in real trouble, Kristen."

Kristen grew more anxious. Sheridan and the police needed to leave. They would see Benito soon. "Tell them it was just a silly accident."

Lucian got out of the car and walked over to the police. His stride was casual and unhurried, as if he had all the time in the world. A young policeman approached him. Within seconds the two were smiling and walking toward the house.

Dane went to greet them.

Sheridan grabbed Kristen by the arm and whispered, "Are you sure you are okay?"

Kristen gave her a shaky smile. "You need to get rid of the police. Crystal is in danger. It has to do with my brother."

"Your brother?"

"I will explain when the police are gone. Please, just hurry. We don't have much time."

Sheridan's eyes narrowed as she studied her. And then, as if coming to a decision, she moved past Kristen outside to the police officers. Within five minutes, she'd convinced the officer that everything was fine.

Dane, Lucian and Sheridan went into the studio lobby. Sheridan closed and locked the front door. She pulled the shades. "Tell me everything, right now, Mr. Cambia."

Dane's lips flattened into a grim line. He clearly didn't like being backed into a corner.

"Tell her," Kristen said.

He glanced at Kristen, then back at Sheridan. "I was FBI until a few weeks ago."

Sheridan shook her head. "I checked all your references."

"That was me you spoke to," Lucian said.

Sheridan met Lucian's gaze. "And who are you?"

"Lucian Moss."

"That tells me exactly nothing." Sheridan's earth-child demeanor had vanished.

Lucian shrugged. "What do you want to know?"

"Start with the basics and then we'll take it from there."

"I do computers."

"That's it?" Sheridan countered.

"Basically, yes."

Sheridan shook her head, facing Dane and Kristen. "Fill me in, now."

Kristen met Sheridan's gaze. "My name is not Kristen Rodale."

Sheridan raised an eyebrow. "No great revelation there."

She wasn't surprised by Sheridan's shrewdness. "My real name is Elena Benito."

"Where have I heard that name before?" Sheridan said.

"It was plastered all over the news nine months ago," Lucian said. He stood leaning against the wall, his arms crossed over his chest.

Sheridan stared at Lucian as the wheels in her memory turned. "Miami. It was a big story from Miami."

Lucian tipped his head toward her. "You get points for that."

Sheridan touched Kristen's short blond hair. "Elena had long beautiful dark hair."

Kristen sighed. "I had to make many changes after the safe house was attacked. I needed to disappear."

Sheridan nodded. "You did a good job of that. The police were baffled. They thought you would be missing forever."

Kristen's jaw tightened. "I would have been if these two men hadn't found me."

Dane stepped forward. "I found Kristen so that I could use her as bait. We needed to draw her brother out."

Sheridan's distaste was clear as her gaze moved between Dane and Lucian. "How very clever of you."

Dane's jaw tightened. He wasn't the kind of man who justified his actions.

"Tell me you have help," Sheridan said.

"It's just us," Dane said.

"It gets worse," Kristen said. "My brother has Crystal."

Silver bracelets jangled on Sheridan's wrist when she dug her fingers through her hair. "She was one of the few at the shelter that I thought would actually get out. She won prizes for her essays. She wanted to go to college."

Tears filled Kristen's eyes. "We will get her back."

"Where is she?" Sheridan said.

"Appletown," Dane said. He checked his watch.

"I know the place," Sheridan said. "I can help."

"We have all the help we need," Lucian said.

Sheridan glanced between Dane and Lucian. "Like it or not, gentlemen, I'm in."

"No." Lucian's voice boomed like a cannon blast.

Dane studied Sheridan. "You don't know what you're saying."

"I've seen my share of trouble, Mr. Cambia," Sheridan said. "And I know how to use a gun."

Chapter 20

Monday, May 21, 8:24 a.m.

With less than minutes to spare, everyone was in place.

Sheridan and Lucian left in his Suburban for Appletown. Their plan was to position themselves in an old mine shaft at the top of the hill that overlooked the old amusement park. The hideout was Sheridan's idea.

That left Kristen and Dane alone to follow in his truck. A heavy silence, as impenetrable as steel, had risen between the two.

Dane broke the silence first. "When this is over, we need to talk."

She lifted her gaze from the worn, cracked leather seat to his eyes. "About what?"

He glanced at her and then back at the road. "Where we go from here?"

"We don't go anywhere from here." Unshed tears constricted her throat, but she refused to cry. "You want my brother and you will have him. And then we will be finished."

"I didn't count on loving you." His voice was a soft whisper.

She raised her hand. "Don't."

He tightened his hands on the steering wheel. "I won't now, but later we will talk."

Neither spoke as they drove out of town. When Dane passed a sign that read Appletown Park 100 Yards, he said, "I want you to stay in the truck until I tell you to come out. I want to keep you as far away from Benito as possible."

Oddly she was very calm. Facing her brother was her fate. She was tired of running. "He won't give you Crystal until he knows I'm there."

"He can see you from inside the truck. I'm trying to buy time until Lucian can get his shot."

"I understand."

A weathered sign reading Appletown hung sideways from a single chain above a dilapidated wooden entrance. A circular go-cart track, eroded by time and rain, had weeds growing up high around a peeling fence that had once encased the track. The old ticket shed had lost its roof and all the go-carts had long since been removed.

Kristen felt as if she'd arrived in a ghost town.

She worried for Crystal, for Sheridan and Lucian and yes, Dane. As angry as she was with Dane, she did not want to see him hurt.

She knew if Benito had his way, none other than she would leave here alive.

Sheridan and Lucian reached the path leading to the abandoned mine shaft on schedule. Silently they climbed out of the Suburban.

From the back hatch, Lucian pulled out a rifle. "So what is this place?"

"There used to be gold mines in the area. This one did well for a time, but it was played out over a century ago."

"The Wild West right here in Virginia."

She hugged her arms around her chest, forcing herself to breathe deeply. "Something like that."

"So where is this rock you were talking about?"

"Over here." She pointed to where it jutted out.

The two climbed through the brush to the outcropping of rock, which was curtained off from the valley below by a stand of trees. Sheridan headed down a narrow path through the woods. Within minutes they reached the edge of the woods and the lip of the overhang.

It provided an excellent view of the valley and a clear shot into Appletown.

Lucian nodded, impressed. "How'd you find out about this place?"

"I grew up in the valley. We used to come up here as kids."

Lucian laid down on the stone surface, as did Sheridan. He took a moment to site the rifle. She winced when he chambered a round.

"Tell me you can handle this," he said without taking his gaze from the valley.

"I can."

He pushed his hair out of his eyes. "I don't want the yoga nonviolence thing to get in the way."

A bitter smile tipped the edge of her full lips. "It won't."

"How do you know?"

Sheridan didn't meet his gaze. "Three years in prison says I can handle just about anything."

Benito stared at the sniveling girl across from him. Crystal was her name. Her jeans were filthy and her hair a revolting shade of blond. It was beyond him why Elena always gravitated toward the strays.

He dropped his gaze to the gold ring on his index finger. Perhaps he needed to change things when he got Elena home. She'd always wanted a dog or a cat. He would choose a pure breed, something classy, like her station dictated. But he would see that she got a pet. That would make her happy. And he wanted her happy.

And he would never expose her to his world again. The violence had been too much for her. He could see that now.

He'd been angry that night in the warehouse. And he'd lost his temper. The murder of those churchmen had been intended to frighten his sister. But he could see now that he'd gone too far.

"What are you going to do with me?" Crystal said.

He glanced up at the girl. He smiled. It would not do for her to get more upset than she already was. "I am going to trade you for my sister."

She sniffed and struggled with the ropes binding her hands behind her back. "You're not going to kill me?"

"Of course not," he lied.

Dane saw the cloud of dirt and dust before he spotted Benito's black Mercedes coming over the rise. Nine months of searching for Benito, countless sleepless nights and a taste for revenge that had never left him would soon be over. Yet the satisfaction was not as sweet as he'd imagined. Black and white had muddled to a gray. He would get Benito but feared he'd lose Kristen.

He touched the 9mm Beretta tucked in his waistband against his spine. Kristen remained in the front cab of his truck. He'd ordered her to stay there until the last second.

The Mercedes stopped and two large men got out of the front seat. They wore black suits and sunglasses. Each held Uzis. One man walked around the back and opened the door. The interior of the car was dark. Dane couldn't see who was inside. But he heard Crystal's sobs. Good. She was still alive.

The goon standing by the back door reached in the car and pulled out Crystal. The girl sported a bruise on the side of her cheek and the sleeve of her jacket was torn. But she could survive that.

Dane turned and opened the van side door. Kristen climbed out of the interior and stood beside him. She had her shoulders back and her chin high, like the princess Benito had raised her to be. But he knew when she stood bolt upright like this, she was afraid. He could feel the tension radiating from her body.

Tense seconds passed as Dane waited for Benito. He thought for a moment the drug dealer wasn't in the car. And then he saw him slide forward and climb out of the vehicle.

Benito's gaze flickered to Kristen. In an instant, relief and joy flashed in his dark eyes before he wiped all traces of emotion from his face. His gaze settled on Dane. Anger radiated from him.

Benito snapped his fingers and one of his men handed him a briefcase. "I believe we agreed on two million dollars."

Dane didn't look to the outcropping of rocks behind him. He needed to draw Benito out farther from the car so that Lucian had a clean shot. Chances were he'd only get one chance.

"Open the briefcase," Dane ordered. "I want to see the money."

Benito raised an amused eye. "Why don't I just have my men kill you now and be done with this mess?"

Dane didn't flinch. "Do you really think I'd walk into this alone?"

Benito's smile faded a fraction. "Ah yes, your computer expert Mr. Lucian, and the yoga instructor."

Dane motioned his hand toward the briefcase. "Is there any money even in the case?"

"Yes."

"Let me see it."

Benito seemed to consider his options. He'd survived as long as he had because he wasn't ruled by impatience. With deliberate grace, he walked to the front of the car and clicked open the gold latches of the case. He lifted the lid. Inside sat rows of tightly packed green bills.

Dane didn't care about the money but he made a point to look at it. After all, this was why he was supposedly here.

"And now my sister," Benito said.

Dane glanced at Benito. He was still out of Lucian's line of sight. He needed to draw him out more.

Kristen seemed to sense this. She was the one who held out her arms to her brother. "Antonio. I want to go home."

The softness of her voice caught her brother's attention. Without thinking, he stepped toward her. Opening her arms, she took a step toward Benito. "Please get me out of here."

Dane stopped Kristen. He wanted her brother to come to her. "First, send Crystal over."

Kristen kept her gaze on her brother. It didn't take much effort to produce the tears in her eyes. She'd never been more afraid in her life. A tear rolled down her cheek. "I want to come home, Antonio."

Benito held out his hand. "You ran from me, my sister. Now return to me."

Like an accomplished actress, anguish and hope filled her eyes on cue. "I was afraid."

Her brother's stern face softened. He liked it when he believed he'd won. "I will never frighten you again, Elena."

Kristen managed a smile.

Benito crossed to her and hugged her close. She wrapped her arms around him and began to weep softly.

Dane didn't dare look toward Lucian, praying he'd wait until Kristen was out of the line of fire.

Benito pulled away and kissed Kristen on the cheek. He looked toward Crystal and then his men. "Kill them all."

Kristen drew back, her face twisted with worry. "You said no more violence."

"I said once we were home. For now, these people must be punished or you will never be safe again." He touched her cheek tenderly.

Dane reached for his Beretta, a sign to Lucian that the situation had gone bad. He whipped his gun around and fired at the first goon, dropping him where he stood. The gunman's Uzi fired wide, sending out a spray of bullets. Crystal screamed and dove to the ground.

Two shots rang out from above the valley. The second gunman dropped to the ground, dead.

Dane shifted his focus to Benito. The drug dealer stumbled back, a blossom of red blood now staining his stomach. The satisfaction Dane felt vanished when he saw Kristen on the ground. She'd been shot in the shoulder and was bleeding badly. The blood on Benito was hers.

Benito's gaze swept over his sister. "Elena!"

Kristen didn't move. She lay on the ground, motionless.

Benito's anger turned from anguish to raw hatred. He stumbled backward to his car and with one last look at his sister closed the car door. The Mercedes sped off.

Dane fired his weapon at the car. He hit the back window, shattering it, but the car kept moving away at top speed.

His choice was simple: Go after Benito or save Kristen.

It was no choice at all for Dane. He lowered his gun and knelt beside Kristen. She was breathing, but losing blood quickly.

He ran toward his van and picked up the walkie-talkie. "Lucian, get a medical helicopter in here now. Kristen's been shot."

Chapter 21

When Kristen awoke in the hospital, the sun was bright and shining through her window. Her body was stiff and her mouth felt dry. An IV ran from her arm. She tried to sit up but found the pain in her shoulder too intense.

"You're awake." Sheridan rose from a chair to her right. Dark smudges marred the skin under her eyes.

"How long have I been out?"

"Four days," Sheridan said. "We were all so

worried. We would have lost you if Dane hadn't gotten you here as fast as he did."

Kristen was glad to hear he was okay, but didn't want to talk about him. It was too painful. "How is Crystal?"

"She's fine." Sheridan picked up a plastic cup with a straw and held it up to Kristen's lips.

She sipped the cool water, savoring the relief in her dry mouth. After the bullet had hit her, she'd lost track of time. "And Antonio?"

She sighed her frustration. "He was shot pretty badly when he got away."

Fear and disappointment collided. "He got away."

Sheridan brushed her bangs off her forehead. "Dane had to choose. You or your brother. He let your brother go so he could save you." She leaned forward. "But don't worry about your brother. State police caught up to him just before the North Carolina border. There was a gun fight. He was killed."

Her brother was dead and, Lord help her, she was glad. Her nightmare was over.

Tears filled Kristen's eyes and spilled down the side of her face. "Where is Dane?"

"No one could pry him out of the hospital until he was certain you were going to be fine. He only left because the FBI had questions." She smiled. "There was a question or two about his undercover operation and a matter of two dead goons to explain."

She didn't want anything bad to happen to Dane. "Is he going to jail?"

"No. Our Mr. Moss rode to his rescue. He has several computer files on organized crime in Florida that the FBI was very interested in acquiring. A deal was struck and no charges were filed and Dane was reinstated in the bureau."

She closed her eyes, suddenly feeling very tired. "Good."

"He loves you, Kristen."

Kristen shook her head. "He gained my trust and used it against me. I never want to see him again."

Sheridan found Dane's truck at the motel, where he'd said he'd be if there was a change in Kristen's condition. She got out of her Bug, marched up to his door and pounded on it.

Almost immediately, curtains flicked back from the window. When he saw that it was her, he opened his door.

He looked like hell. His eyes were bloodshot and dark circles hung under each. Sheridan doubted he'd slept since the shooting five days ago.

"Is Kristen all right?" he asked.

She noticed the suitcase on the bed. It was half-packed. "She's fine. Where are you going?"

"I've been reassigned."

"So, you're just leaving?" she snapped. "What about Kristen? Are you just going to abandon her?"

He glared. "She doesn't want to see me anymore. She made that very clear."

"That's crap. She was upset. Her feelings were too raw."

"I betrayed her, Sheridan. She's got reason to hate me."

"That doesn't mean that she doesn't love you. She needs you now more than ever."

Hope flickered and died in his eyes. "She's got you. You'll take good care of her."

"Yeah, I would take damn good care of her. But you're the one that she loves. You're the one that she needs."

He sank down onto the bed as if all the fight and energy in him had drained away. "I don't know how to make things right."

"For such a big tough guy, you are a soft touch when it comes to Kristen."

"That's right."

"You need to go to her. You need to tell her you love her until she finally hears you. You've got to win her heart all over again."

He was out of his depth. "I don't think I know how."

She smiled. "You'll figure it out."

* * *

The basket arrived in Kristen's hospital room that afternoon. It was white wicker and lined with a red-checked table cloth. Inside it were two rolled up beach towels, a bottle of suntan lotion, a Merlot, two crystal glasses and a large and very expensive box of chocolates.

Kristen was sitting up when the nurse set the basket on the table beside her hospital bed. Crystal, who was sitting in a chair by the window, scrambled to her feet. Her eyes danced with youthful excitement. "What is this?"

Kristen reached for the white envelope. On it was her name written in a bold script. She opened the envelope and read the card.

"What does it say?" Crystal practically danced with excitement. It amazed Kristen how well the girl had rebounded. She'd moved out of the youth shelter and in with Sheridan at the studio. Sheridan had petitioned the courts for custody.

"The card says, '*For That Perfect Day. Dane*.'"

Crystal pulled out the box of chocolates. "Can I have a piece?"

Kristen smiled. "Sure."

The girl opened the box and bit into a nut cluster. She smiled with pleasure. "The man sure does know his chocolate."

Kristen laid the card on the table. "I suppose."

"Didn't he send you a basket filled with gourmet popcorn and about a million DVDs, too?"

"Yes."

Crystal popped the rest of the chocolate into her mouth. "The man is so in love with you that I bet he can't see straight."

She wiped a tear from her cheek. "He doesn't love me. He might feel guilt, but not love."

Crystal started to dance around and sing, "He is your *boy-friend*. I think he *loves* you."

Sheridan breezed into the room as Crystal started to sing her song again. "What's this?"

"Dane sent Kristen another basket. He l-loves *her.*"

Sheridan smiled as she inspected the basket. "I'd say you are right."

Kristen shook her head. "I don't want these things. He used me."

Sheridan sat beside her bed. She took Kristen's hand in hers. "Yes, he did. But sometimes you've got to do something that is awful to save others. Your brother had to be stopped."

Kristen didn't deny that. "If he'd told me what he needed, I would have helped."

"He didn't know that. All he knew was that you were on the run. He couldn't take the chance. The stakes were too high."

Crystal ate another piece of chocolate. "The guy looks like hell, Kristen. Give him a second chance."

At that moment the door opened. Dane walked in. He'd shaved, showered and brushed back his newly cut black hair. He wore khakis and a button-down shirt. She hardly recognized the man who'd come into her life just over a week ago.

But Lord, did he look good. Sheridan and Crystal glanced at each other. On cue, they picked up their stuff and left the room.

Kristen sat up. She wanted nothing more than to take him in her arms and hold him close. "Thank you for the basket."

"You're welcome." He picked the basket up and set it on a side table so that he could see her better. "Kristen, I am sorry."

"I know."

"I love you."

The words sliced through the heart of her resolve to be strong. She nodded, unable to speak through the emotion.

"I was offered my job back with the FBI. It'll mean being reassigned to the West Coast."

She nodded. "I am glad for you."

"I chose San Diego because it has warm beaches."

A tear spilled down her cheek. She felt too emotional to speak.

"I want you to come with me." He pulled a black velvet box from his pocket and handed it to her.

"What is this?"

"Open it."

The box's hinges squeaked when she did. Inside there was a square emerald ring. "It's lovely."

"It's meant to be a ring of commitment and when and if you're ready, an engagement ring. I don't want to rush you, Kristen. You have lost so much time and have so much living in front of you, and I won't stand in the way of that. But I hope you'll forgive me and come with me to San Diego."

She'd known Dane such a short time and they'd been through so much, but she knew in her heart that she loved him. She pulled the ring out of the velvet pillow and slipped it on the ring finger of her left hand. "I love you."

The strained tension in his face vanished and he smiled his relief. He leaned forward and gently kissed her on the lips. He tasted so good.

The sadness drained from her body. She wrapped her arms around his neck and pulled herself closer to him. She savored his scent and his touch.

"I love you," he whispered against her lips.

Kristen knew that no matter where they were, as long as she was with him, she was home.

Epilogue

One Year Later

It was Kristen's wedding day.

And she was late.

The world history book weighted down Kristen's backpack as she hurried through the back door of the house she shared with Dane.

Lord, it seemed she was always late these days. There was so much to do, so much to cram into her days. The world had so many possibilities now.

She'd fully intended to spend her wedding day

dressing and primping but then she'd been invited to a lecture from a visiting professor. Only the top students had been invited. It was a great honor for her.

Dane had insisted she go. So she had.

And now she was late on the worst day of all to be late. At three o'clock she and Dane were going to be married in the small chapel overlooking the sea.

And Lord, but she adored Dane.

Her dog, Trixie, a ten-year-old lab mix, looked up from her doggie bed and thumped her tail against the floor. She and Dane had rescued the dog from a shelter six months ago.

Kristen patted the dog on the head, dumped her backpack on the kitchen table and kicked off her shoes before hurrying toward the bedroom. She heard the shower running and knew it was Dane. She smiled. If she had her way, she'd slip into the shower with him.

She checked her watch. If she hurried, she could be ready in fifteen minutes. They'd only be a half hour late to the private ceremony they'd scheduled with the parish priest.

After pulling her shirt off she tossed it on the hallway floor, expecting to see the wedding dress she'd laid out this morning on her bed. It was. And so were the three black kittens she'd found last week. They were nestled together on the center of the dress.

Kristen stopped, groaned.

Dane came out of the shower. He wore a towel around his narrow waist. Water glistened from the thick mat of hair on his chest. "As you can see, the girls have made themselves at home."

She grimaced and gently picked a sleeping kitten up. Black hair covered the spot where she'd been lying. "I will never get this dress cleaned in time."

Dane took the kitten from Kristen and set it back on the bed. Immediately, the kitten crawled back to her spot on the dress.

Dane's gaze dropped to Kristen's cleavage. The desire in his expression made her blood warm. Suddenly she wasn't in such a rush to leave the house.

He traced the curve of her breasts with his fingertip.

"We will be late," she said, reading his thoughts.

"I already called the minister and told him we'd be there in an hour. We've got time."

She wrapped her arms around his neck. "I wanted to be beautiful for you today."

He ran his hands through her dark layered hair, which had grown out to her shoulders. "You are stunning as always. It doesn't matter what you wear."

She tugged at his towel and dropped it to the floor.

He glanced at the kittens, picked her up and carried her to the spare room. He kicked the door closed and laid her on the bed.

They made it to the church. And they were on time, just barely. Kristen wore a lemon sundress and the minister said he'd never seen a lovelier bride.

* * * * *

**Hidden in the secrets of antiquity,
lies the unimagined truth...**

Introducing

a brand-new line filled with mystery
and suspense, action and adventure,
and a fascinating look into history.

And it all begins with DESTINY.

In a sealed crypt in
France, where the
terrifying legend of
the beast of Gevaudan
begins to unravel,
Annja Creed discovers
a stunning artifact
that will seal her destiny.

*Available every other
month starting
July 2006, wherever
you buy books.*

Page-turning drama...

Exotic, glamorous locations...

Intense emotion and passionate seduction...

Sheikhs, princes and billionaire tycoons...

This summer, may we suggest:

THE SHEIKH'S DISOBEDIENT BRIDE
by Jane Porter

On sale June.

AT THE GREEK TYCOON'S BIDDING
by Cathy Williams

On sale July.

THE ITALIAN MILLIONAIRE'S VIRGIN WIFE

On sale August.

With new titles to choose from every month, discover a world of romance in our books written by internationally bestselling authors.

It's the ultimate in quality romance!

Available wherever Harlequin books are sold.

www.eHarlequin.com

HPGEN06

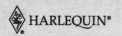

If you enjoyed what you just read,
then we've got an offer you can't resist!

Take 2 bestselling
love stories FREE!
Plus get a FREE surprise gift!

COMING NEXT MONTH

#1427 SOMEBODY'S HERO—Marilyn Pappano
Recently divorced Jayne Miller moves to the small town of
Sweetwater, where she plans to revive her career as a romance
author…and it doesn't hurt to have a handsome, brooding
neighbor for inspiration. Tyler Lewis isn't happy to have
neighbors, but no matter how much he refutes his desires,
Jayne makes him want what he can't have…not with the
secrets in his past.

#1428 MORE THAN A MISSION—Caridad Piñeiro
Capturing the Crown
When undercover agent Aidan Spaulding is asked to investigate
the murder of Prince Reginald, he is given the chance to identify
the Sparrow—the infamous female assassin who killed his best
friend. All signs point to Elizabeth Moore, a local restaurant
owner, but as Aidan gets to know the refreshingly kind woman, he
realizes there is no way she is the assassin. But if Elizabeth isn't
the Sparrow, who is?

#1429 BAPTISM IN FIRE—Elizabeth Sinclair
Two years ago, arson investigator Rachel Sutherland's home
went up in flames, followed by her marriage to Detective
Luke Sutherland when they were unable to find either their
daughter or the fire starter. Now divorced, they must join forces
against a serial arsonist—the same one who destroyed their
dreams. Could they rebuild in time to find the firebug—and
possibly their child?

#1430 DEADLY MEMORIES—Susan Vaughan
Sophie Rinaldi is researching her ancestors in Italy when
she overhears plans of a terrorist attack in her host's mansion.
Barely escaping death, she turns to U.S. Marshal Jack Thorne
for help and finds comfort in his steady gaze. They get swept
up in a dangerous attraction, which Jack tries to temper
during his investigation. Can Jack keep his vow to capture
his enemy without jeopardizing the life of the only woman
he will ever love?